Voyager II—
Back in a Flash!

Voyager II—
Back in a Flash!

Charles Mills

Review and Herald® Publishing Association
Washington, DC 20039-0555
Hagerstown, MD 21740

The author assumes full responsibility for the accuracy of all facts and quotations as cited in this book.

This book was
Edited by Jeannette Johnson
Designed by Bill Kirstein
Cover photo by Meylan Thoresen

PRINTED IN U.S.A.

96 95 94 93 92 91   10 9 8 7 6 5 4 3 2 1

R&H Cataloging Service
Mills, Charles Henning, 1950-
Voyager II—Back in a flash!

Sequel to Voyager: the book.
I. Title.

ISBN 0-8280-0595-8

To Dorinda
my friend . . .
my partner . . .
my wife

Contents

Home

"TESTING, testing, one, two, three, testing."
Tony watched the volume indicator needle on his cassette tape recorder dance with each word he spoke into the microphone. "This is Tony Parks, testing, testing."

Carefully, he adjusted small, round control knobs, searching for the setting that would assure a clear recording with no hint of distortion.

"Coming to you live from the Parks farm, it's the Tony Show, with your host, Tony Parks!" The boy forced air along his throat, trying to mimic the sound of thunderous applauding and cheering. Closing his eyes, he imagined himself surrounded by state-of-the-art broadcasting equipment with millions of admiring fans sitting by their radios excitedly awaiting his every word.

"Thank you, thank you!" Tony returned their adoration.

"You welcome, you welcome." Startled, the would-be announcer looked up to discover Tie Li standing in the doorway.

"Oh, you scared me, little sister. How long have you been there?"

"I just come now. I thought you listening to the radio."

Tony brightened. "You did? You thought I was the radio?"

"Yes. You sound like someone I hear all the time."

Pride filled the boy's chest. "I do? Who?"

"That man who sells cars and sits on a horse. I see him on TV too."

Tony's smile faded. "You don't mean Wild Bill Branson, the used-car salesman? He's terrible! He sounds like a goat."

"But he have very nice horse."

The boy sighed and lifted his hands to his head. "My career is ended. I'm crushed."

Tie Li walked over to her brother. "I just kidding, Tony. You sound much better. You sound like newsman on TV."

Tony looked through his fingers. "Are you just saying that to make me feel better?"

"Yes. I mean no. I mean—I'm confused." Tie Li threw her hands up in frustration. "If you had radio program, I'd listen to you every day. I promise."

Tony burst out laughing. "It's OK, Tie Li. I know you would. But I'm going to have to wait till my voice changes before I audition for the networks. For now, I just like to pretend."

The girl nodded. "Me too. Sometimes I pretend I'm a doctor, and I help people who get hurt. I go back to my country when the war is gone. I make everybody well and happy again."

Tie Li sat down slowly beside Tony. "People can get well and happy again, can't they?"

"You bet, Tie Li. But sometimes they need more help than a doctor can give."

"Like Kim?"

The boy nodded. "Yes."

Tie Li traced a design on her skirt with her finger. "Will man in city help him?"

Tony looked down at his sister. "I think so. If anyone can, he can. That's what Mom and Dad say."

The two sat in silence for a long moment. Suddenly Tony jumped to his feet. "Aren't we forgetting something?"

Tie Li jumped up too. "Yes. What?"

"Simon Gorby. We're supposed to be making a tape to send him, remember?"

A smile returned to the girl's face. "Yes, yes! We make a tape right now, OK?"

Tony motioned toward his desk. "The recorder is ready to go. I put a brand-new tape in it."

The two sat down in front of a microphone Tony propped up on his study desk. The boy punched a few buttons and then, with professional poise, pointed at Tie Li.

Taking a deep breath, the girl began to speak.

"Hi, Simon. This your friend Tie Li talking. Thank you for sending me and Tony a letter. I read it five times already.

"I hope you like your new home in Florida. It's nice that you live near the beach and can go swimming a lot. I don't think you want to go swimming here. Last night it snowed six inches.

"Do you know what? My brother Kim is not—is not dead. He alive! He came on the airplane." Tie Li's voice faltered. "I see him at the airport. I—"

Tony leaned toward the microphone. "That's true,

11

Simon. We were there to meet Sister Martinez and a bunch of other kids from Tie Li's country, and there he was. Boy, was it a shock!

"He speaks real good English—better than you. Government schools must be tough.

"Mom and Dad said we could adopt him, too, just like we adopted Tie Li. Hey, Simon, I've got a brother who can beat you up. *Now* he shows!" Tony laughed out loud. "Where was he when I needed him?"

Tie Li joined in. "His bed is in attic room. He has little window, and can see the barn and pastures. He likes to sit by window and watch the cows.

"Sometimes I sit with him. I tell him about the farm and about how I fell in Bentley's Pond and how Tony and I helped the chipmunk. But he doesn't talk very much. He just listens to me. I think he's very sad.

"I ask him to come play with Tony and me. He says he's tired. When I'm building a snowman in the yard I look up at the window and I see him there watching me. I wave. Sometimes he waves to me too.

"Mom and Dad took him to a special man in the city. He's like a doctor, but doesn't do operations and stuff like that. They say he will help my brother feel better. I hope so. I love him and want him to be happy, the way he was before the war came to our village. This his home now. Here on farm. The other home is gone. Now he live here with me and Tony." The girl hesitated. "I don't know why he so sad. Why doesn't he play with me like before?"

Tie Li's voice drifted into silence. Tony quietly reached over and pressed a button on the recorder. With a *click* the tape stopped turning. The girl looked up at her brother. "Why, Tony? Why doesn't he play with me?"

Tony stood up and walked to the window by his bed. His

12

room was right below Kim's. He could see the barnyard and pastures spreading out under the new snow. At the corner of the barn was the door to his workshop. Could his invention help Kim? Tony wondered. Would the man in the garden, the baby in the manger, help a boy with so much hurt inside? He stood staring into the cold afternoon air.

Far from the farm, amid the towering steel fingers of the city, another face stared from a window high above the throbbing streets. Lines of frustration appeared on the man's forehead as he studied the skyline. Taking a deep breath, he spoke with controlled agitation. "How am I supposed to help you if you refuse to talk to me?" He turned and looked at the 13-year-old boy sitting hunched down in the big overstuffed chair across the room.

"Look, I'm not trying to embarrass you. I don't want you to feel uncomfortable. I'm just trying to help. But you've got to talk to me, tell me what's going on inside that head of yours."

The boy looked at the man by the window. "What's it to you? Why do you have to know everything about me? My name is Kim. My home is a burned-out hole in the ground in a country far away from here. What else matters?"

The psychiatrist hurried to his desk. "A lot more matters. I know your past is painful, terribly so. But you have a future, a new home, people who want to love you. And you have a sister who needs you very, very much."

Kim jumped to his feet. "What do you know about it? Have you ever had soldiers burn your village to the ground? Have you seen your parents—?" The boy fought to control his emotions. "You don't know what it's like. No one knows. No one!"

Kim buried his face in his fists. A groan escaped

between clinched teeth. "I don't have a home anymore. I don't belong anywhere. Just leave me alone!"

The doctor closed his eyes. A familiar anger rose in his heart. Innocent victims were the worst casualties of war. Sometimes the mind suffered the most. And the mind was the hardest to heal.

He watched the boy rock back and forth in the chair. How do you create a home for the homeless? How do you return love to someone who has seen it snatched from him so violently?

"I cannot leave you alone in your suffering, Kim," he said quietly. "For every person who hates in this world, there's someone who's willing to love."

Kim looked over at the doctor. "You're wrong. All love burned up in my village."

Promises to Keep

TONY'S fingers flew over the keyboard of his computer. The clickety-clack of the keys punctuated the
whine from the little electric heater in the corner.
Out of its metallic mouth a gentle breath of warm air flowed
over the woodworking tools and assorted piles of integrated
circuits, computer parts, handwritten plans, and detailed
diagrams scattered in organized chaos on the top of Tony's
workbench.

Every once in a while the boy would stop and study the
neat rows of words and numbers radiating in the soft amber
glow of his computer screen. He'd chew on his bottom lip
for a moment, then continue typing.

His invention sat heavily against the wall opposite the
workbench. The tall wooden box with its forest of antennae,
stacks of control panels, blinking lights, four metal cylinders, and maze of wiring gave the machine a battered and
disorganized look.

The battered parts had fallen victim to "nonstandard
operations," as Tony called their close encounter with
Noah's ark. Other portions of the invention had been

labeled as "Simonized". Tie Li giggled whenever Tony referred to a broken lead or bent support frame using that word.

During the past few days, *Voyager* had been stripped down to its bare essentials, then, with painstaking attention to detail, put back together again. New parts had arrived in the mail. The boy hoped his calculations had been correct. He was running out of money. Last summer's part-time job had earned him only so much.

"Tony?" Mr. Parks poked his head into the workshop. "I'm going to town. You need anything?"

"Uh . . . no . . . not today, Dad. Thanks for asking." Tony smiled at his father. "You taking Kim with you?"

"He said he didn't want to go. I guess he gets kinda tired of sitting in the car during our weekly trip to visit Dr. McFerren in the city. Can't say that I blame him. It is a long trip."

Tony stretched stiff muscles and turned a knob to darken the image on his screen. "Dad, can I ask you something?"

Mr. Parks entered the workshop and closed the door behind him. "Sure, son. I don't know if I'll have the answer, but I'll try."

Tony watched his father brush snow from his coat. He really liked his dad. A lot of kids at school talked down about their fathers. But Tony respected his. He knew his dad would be honest with him no matter what. He also knew his father would never try to cover up what he didn't know. Truth had a security about it, even when it wasn't what a guy wanted to hear.

Tony faced Mr. Parks. "What can I do to help Kim? I'm his brother. I feel like I should be doing something, but I don't know what."

The man sighed. "I don't know what to tell you, son.

Kim is . . . hurting inside. He's afraid to let others close to him because he thinks they'll be taken away. At least that's what Dr. McFerren says."

Tony scratched his head thoughtfully. "I'm not going to go away. Tie Li isn't either. You and Mom are adopting him. Why won't he believe we all love him and want him to be a part of our family?"

Mr. Parks nodded in agreement. "But we have to remember he had another family once. I'm sure his father promised he'd never leave, and that the family would always be together, come what may. But sometimes life has a cruel way of breaking the strongest promises. Now Kim's withdrawn into himself. He figures if he doesn't need anybody, he can't be hurt again."

The boy was quiet for a moment, then spoke slowly. "I'm lucky, aren't I? I have a great mom and dad, a neat farm to live on, my computer, and a wonderful sister, too. Why do I have it so good while other people suffer so much?"

Mr. Parks studied his son's face. "I don't know, Tony. I don't have an answer for that question. I guess there are some things we weren't meant to understand."

The man turned to leave, then hesitated. "Tony, I don't mean to make it sound like promises aren't worth anything. To an honest man, a promise is as important as breathing. But things happen. Even honest men can't control life and death.

"Kim is a member of our family now. Our responsibility is to keep the promises his first dad made to him." The man's tone became firm. "Some things even war can't take away."

Mr. Parks quietly closed the door behind him as he left. Tony sat in the stillness, listening to his father's footsteps

17

crunching on the packed snow outside the door. As the sound faded, the boy let out a long sigh, then turned back to his computer and began typing again.

Tie Li sat at the kitchen table watching her mother roll bread dough into gooey mounds. Rows of shiny pans waited nearby, ready to accept their loads for the oven.

The little girl's chin rested on her folded hands. Blotches of white flour covered her brown cheeks and forehead. Even her long, dark hair was decorated with powdery highlights.

"I like bread," she said, sticking her finger into the large mound beside her elbow. "First you play with it, then you eat it. It lots of fun."

Mrs. Parks looked down at her helper. "Which do you like better, playing or eating?"

Tie Li rubbed her chin, absentmindedly applying another layer of flour to her face. "That a hard decision. When I play, I get hungry. When I eat, I get energy to play."

"What about studying and going to school? Don't you like doing that, too?"

The girl looked up at her mother. "Is there school where I can just play and eat?"

Mrs. Parks laughed. "I don't think so."

Tie Li sighed and examined her dough encrusted finger. "Too bad. I'd get all A's there."

Before long, the fresh smell of baking bread filled the big yellow farmhouse. The afternoon passed quickly. Kitchens and cooking held almost as much fascination for the little girl as Tony and his workshop. But Tony had asked Tie Li to let him work alone on rebuilding *Voyager*. She knew how hard he concentrated when he was busy with an invention. Tie Li had readily agreed to keep out of sight.

She was eager for the machine to be back in working order.

As evening shadows crept across the farmyard, Mrs. Parks asked Tie Li to find Tony and Kim and tell them to get ready for supper. The girl scurried up the stairs to the second floor. In the hallway, she stopped at the foot of the stairs leading to Kim's attic room.

"Kim? Kim! Time to eat supper. I make a big loaf of bread for you. You're gonna like it. Kim?" Tie Li waited for a response. "Kim? You up there?"

No voice answered from the top of the stairs. The girl started climbing the wooden passageway. "Hey, Kim. You sleeping?" Rounding the top of the stairs, Tie Li stopped in her tracks. The room had been torn apart. Clothes and papers littered the floor. The dresser lay tilted on its side. Glass from the broken mirror glistened from the folds of a rug pushed into the corner. Tie Li stepped back in horror. Stumbling down the attic stairs, she hurried into Tony's room. Opening the window, she screamed into the frigid air, "Tony! Tony! Come quick!"

The door to the workshop burst open as Tony rushed into the yard. He looked up toward his window. "What is it, Tie Li? What's the matter?"

Mrs. Parks raced up the stairs and ran to Tony's room. "Tie Li, what's happened? What's going on?"

The girl stood trembling, tears leaving long, floury stains on her cheeks.

Tony sped up the stairs two at a time. "Tie Li, why are you crying? What's the matter?"

The little girl pushed past him and ran down the hall to the stairway leading to the attic. Mrs. Parks and Tony followed close behind. They all reached Kim's room at the same time.

The woman's breath caught in her throat as she saw

what was left of the attic room. Tony let out a low whistle. "What in the world happened here? It looks like someone tried to destroy this whole room."

Tie Li sat down on the top stair, her hands over her eyes. "Where my brother?" she cried. "Where Kim?"

Tony noticed a piece of paper impaled on a nail where a picture used to hang. He walked over to it, trying not to step on the broken glass littering the floor. "Look, there's writing on this."

Tony handed the note to his mother. Bending close to the overturned lamp, she read the words scrawled across it.

"I can't stay here. Don't try to find me."

Tie Li bolted down the stairs and ran back to Tony's open window. "Kim!" she screamed toward the pastures. "Kim, come back. Don't go away again. Come back. *Please, come back!*"

The wind lifted her cries from the warm light of the window and carried them over the barnyard, into the darkness.

The Cabin

TONY jammed his feet into his thick hiking boots, grabbed his scarf from the hook on the wall, and wound it tightly around his neck. In two swift movements he slipped his gloves over his hands and headed for the back door.

"I'll find him, Tie Li," he called over his shoulder, trying to sound encouraging. "I know the pastures and forests around here better than he does. I'll find him; don't worry."

A cold blast of wind hit the boy as he opened the door. Another storm was brewing. He must find and follow Kim's tracks before new snow covered them up. Time was not on his side.

Mrs. Parks shouted into the wind. "Be careful, Tony! When your father gets home I'll tell him what's happened. He'll start searching too." The woman's voice was strained. "Just be careful!"

Stopping by his workshop, Tony retrieved his big flashlight from its recharging stand. The bright beam shot out into the darkness, revealing blowing white drifts and an

21

ever-increasing amount of falling snow.

He searched the edges of the yard, looking for signs in the powdery mounds. By the big birch he found tracks leading through the split-rail fence, heading in the direction of the south pasture.

They belonged to Kim. He was sure. No one else would be going out that way this time of year.

Tony eased through the fence and started following the footprints in the snow, his mind filling with questions. *Why would Kim run away? Why would he leave a warm house and head out into the cold like this? And what about Tie Li?*

The boy felt anger rising deep inside him. Kim hadn't even considered how this would affect Tie Li. *She loves him! Never mind what he thinks of Mom and Dad, much less me. But Tie Li. She's his sister! Doesn't he care about her at all?*

Tony quickened his pace. The wind seemed to blow straight through his layers of clothes. A chill ran down the back of his neck.

The tracks wound through the south pasture, turned east, and followed the edge of the woods by the Bentley farm. As Tony crested the top of a small rise, his breath caught in his throat. The tracks were heading straight for the pond. In the darkness, and with so much snow on the ground, Kim wouldn't have known the pond existed. He could have walked right out to the middle, thinking he was still on dry land.

Tony stumbled along, fearful of what he might find. The bright beam of the flashlight illuminated the tracks as Tony hurried down the hill. Had the surface frozen enough to hold Kim's weight, or would the tracks end in a black, wet hole out in the middle of Bentleys' Pond?

At the edge where Tony knew the water would be,

Kim's tracks continued straight ahead. Tony turned and followed the shoreline, keeping the trail leading out onto the pond in range of his flashlight. He held his breath. Kim's path was leading him over 25 feet of cold, dark water.

Tony stumbled and slid, trying to keep his footing on the uneven edge of the snow-covered body of water, his flashlight steadily scanning Kim's progress.

"Please don't break! Please don't break!" Tony repeated the words over and over to himself.

After what seemed like an agonizing eternity, the tracks grew closer and closer to where Tony stumbled along. Then they were underfoot. "He made it!" the boy shouted into the wind. "All *right!*"

Tony sat down on the bank. He could breathe again. The ice had held Kim's weight all the way across. He sat for a long moment, following the tracks over the pond with the bright beam of his flashlight until they disappeared into the darkness. *You're one lucky guy, Kim,* he thought to himself. *You don't know how lucky you are.*

Tony shook his head slowly from side to side. *Somebody's watching out for you, that's all I can say.*

The boy remembered the multitude crossing the Red Sea. He saw the ark sitting battered, but intact, on the boulders, high in the barren mountains. A thought flickered in the back of his mind. Could it be? But that was so long ago. Did He still do that kind of stuff today?

Tony rose to his feet. The tracks led up the hill, toward the trees. Getting his bearing, the boy began to follow them. Kim had to be told. He had to know about the pond, about the ark, about the man in the garden.

But how? Kim didn't trust anyone. He wouldn't listen.

At the edge of the woods, Tony stopped. The wind

blowing through the trees carried a particular scent. It smelled like—like—

The boy looked up in surprise. The cabin! Why hadn't he thought of that before? Kim had made it to the cabin!

A fresh determination sped Tony along. Several years before, he and his dad had built a cabin deep in the woods. It was sort of a little getaway, a place to camp on warm summer nights.

Tony began to run. The smell of burning logs meant Kim had built a fire to keep himself warm. Stepping into a clearing, Tony shone his flashlight in the direction of a small wooden structure nestled among the trees on the far side. Sure enough, a soft, yellow glow spilled from the windows and formed pools of light on the snow. Smoke curled from the chimney and hurried away with the wind.

Tony stood looking at the cabin for a moment. What should he say to his new brother? Would Kim try to chase him away?

Snow began to fall in earnest as the wind built to a roar. Tony spoke softly to himself. "It's too late now. Like it or not, he's got company for the night. I'm not heading back in this storm."

The boy made his way to the front of the cabin. Drawing in a deep breath, he lifted the latch and pushed open the door. The warm glow from the fireplace cast long, willowy shadows across the room. Kim looked up, startled by the burst of cold air that followed Tony into the room.

"What are you doing here?" he said, pulling a blanket closer about him. "I told everybody to leave me alone."

Tony brushed snow from his pants and coat. "I know." He sat down on a chair to pull off his ice-encrusted boots. "Tie Li was worried. She was scared something might happen to you. And you better believe that something almost did!''

"Who cares?'' Kim looked back into the fire.

Tony felt the anger rising again. He almost shouted. "Tie Li cares! Mom and Dad care!'' Softening, he added, "I guess I care too.''

Kim continued to stare into the flames. He spoke quietly. "I love my sister.''

"You sure have a crazy way of showing it. And what did you tear up your room for? What's the matter with you, anyway?''

Kim covered his ears with his hands. "I don't want to talk about it, all right? I'm confused. I'm angry. I don't know what to think or how to act. I just want to—to—oh, never mind.''

Tony's mouth dropped open. "You want to die, don't you? Isn't that what you're trying to say?''

Kim spun around, his face flushed with frustration. *"Yes!* I want to die! There, I've said it. Now leave me *alone!''* The boy buried his face in his hands, great sobs rocking his body.

Tony jumped to his feet. "Why? Why, Kim? I know you had a horrible past, but why do you want to die?''

"Because.'' The words were choked. "Because I can't live with the pain. It's too much. Every minute, every second, I remember my village, my parents, the way it used to be. Each day the hurt is worse than before. I just can't live with it anymore.

"I feel guilty because I can't be a good brother to Tie Li. I see her looking at me with such love, and I can't return it. I hate myself. I'm no good to anybody. Everything I love gets destroyed. I'm even afraid to love Tie Li. Something would probably happen to her.'' He looked over at Tony.

"But I love her so much. I love her . . ." The boy's voice faltered in a long, painful cry. He buried his face in the blanket and leaned against the pile of firewood resting beside him.

Tony stood in the shadows, trying to understand the depth of his brother's sorrow. In a world of computers and mathematics, problems all have logical, well-defined methods for getting solved. But here was a broken heart. How did you fix that?

"Kim?" Tony walked across the room and sat down beside the sobbing boy. "I'm sorry you're so sad. I don't understand everything you say. I've never lost as much as you have. But . . ." Tony searched for words, "I think I can show you Someone who has. Maybe He can help you understand how to live and be happy again. But it's a secret. Only Tie Li and I know about it, and you have to promise you won't tell anybody."

Kim raised his head. "What are you talking about?"

Tony hesitated. "You've got to promise me you won't tell a soul."

"All right, all right, I promise."

"OK. Now listen. Out in my workshop—"

The door to the cabin burst open as Mr. Parks rushed in. "Tony? Kim?" He saw the boys sitting by the fire. Heaving a great sigh of relief, he sat down heavily on a nearby chair. "Thank God you two are all right. I thought you'd probably head up this way. The snow has covered your tracks. Kim, you gave us quite a scare. Are you OK?"

Kim shook his head. "I'm OK."

Tony stood and walked over to his father. "Dad, can we stay here tonight, Kim and I? We need to talk about some stuff."

The man studied his son's face. "Well, I guess so. The

fire will keep you warm. You sure you'll be all right?''

''We'll be fine, Dad. Thanks for coming to look for us.''

''If that's what you want. I know a little girl who's about to climb the walls down at the farm. She'll be glad to know you two are safe and sound. You both mean a lot to her.'' He looked at Kim. ''You know that, don't you?''

The boy nodded and looked away.

Mr. Parks rose to leave. ''I'll see you guys in time for breakfast, OK?''

Tony waved. ''We'll be there.''

The man walked into the night, following the beam of his flashlight. The storm had begun to slacken. Occasionally the moon would peek from behind high clouds, flooding the world in softness. What was Tony talking about? What was so important back there in the cabin?

Nazareth

THIS IS it? This is your great invention?'' Kim studied the tall box standing in the corner of Tony's workshop. ''You gotta be kidding!''

The older boy walked over to the door of *Voyager* and opened it. He stared at the colorful rows of knobs, lights, levers, switches, and dials. Computer screens, maps, and charts covered the back inside wall of the machine, while a collection of control panels and system indicator boards crowded the sides.

Tony joined him. ''Neat, huh? It may not look like much, but it works.''

Kim backed away. ''No way. You're not getting me in that thing.''

''Come on, Kim, it's safe. I built it very carefully. It's even had a whole bunch of improvements made on it since its last trip.''

''What do your folks say about this?''

Tony looked over at his brother. ''They don't believe it does what I say it does. They think I'm just playing a game with Tie Li. That's OK with me. They don't worry.''

"Worry? Worry about what?"

"Oh, you know what I mean. Parents just worry all the time. Must be part of their job."

Kim looked unconvinced. "It still makes me a little nervous." Tie Li entered the workshop and closed the door behind her. She stopped when she saw Kim standing beside *Voyager*. Her eyes searched Tony's.

"It's OK," Tony said. "I told him about it last night at the cabin."

Tie Li glanced at Kim, then back at Tony. "You told him everything?"

Tony nodded. "Everything."

The girl's face lightened into a smile. "Then you come too, Kim?"

Kim took in a deep breath. "Well, I—I guess so."

Tie Li raced across the room and threw herself into her brother's arms. "I so glad you'll come, Kim. Now you can meet the man in the garden. Now you can see many wonderful things. I very excited!"

Kim looked over at Tony. The older boy's eyes still reflected uncertainty. But Tony noticed that when Kim spoke to Tie Li, there was a spark of love in his voice. Maybe it wasn't too late. Maybe Kim could learn to understand, to accept, to live.

"Then it's settled. From now on, we'll all go." Tony closed the door of his invention. Something had been added to the name painted in bright red-letters across the front. "Welcome to *Voyager II*," Tony said proudly.

Tie Li clapped her delight. "We go together; we go together." She danced around the room, not trying to contain her happiness. Her brother had made his first step into her new world, their new world.

Tony opened the door again. "Come on, you guys, it's

time to go! You get in *Voyager* first, Kim.''

He directed Kim to stand against the back right-hand corner of the box. He'd built support holds at just the right level for the older boy to hold on to. "I've been planning this for a few weeks," he admitted weakly. "I was hoping I'd get you to join us.''

Tie Li unfolded her little bench from the inside wall and took her faithful football helmet off the hook on the back of the door. Looking up at Kim, she said meekly, "When you little, you get bumped.''

Kim nodded, still not convinced he'd made the right decision.

Tony squeezed in next, his back to Tie Li and Kim. Closing the door, he spoke in the darkness. *"Voyager,* power up.''

Lights sparkled on all over the inside walls of the machine. A low hum vibrated the floor under the children's feet.

Tony's hands moved about the control panels, adjusting knobs, flicking switches, and pressing buttons. A computer screen blinked on above his head. Looking up, Tony studied the numbers and symbols illuminated there. Folding down a keyboard at his waist, the boy typed in a command. The screen responded by listing the destinations Tony had entered in his data base the day before.

Kim scanned the words. He'd never heard of any of them. **BETHEL, CANA, CAPERNAUM, GALILEE, OLIVET.** His lips moved silently, trying to pronounce each one. **SAMARIA, JORDAN, TIBERIAS.**

Tony punched a few more keys, and a new list appeared, filled with words that were strange and mysterious. Kim saw his brother bring the on-screen selector down through rows until it stopped on a word near the bottom. The boy leaned forward to read the letters **NAZARETH**.

Tony reached above his head and pulled a lever. A circuit somewhere on *Voyager* switched off the magnetic field holding the four outboard cable connectors in place. The leads running from the metal cylinders at the four corners of the machine dropped from their attach plates and clattered to the floor.

Bright-red letters appeared on the screen above Tony's head. **POWER ON INTERNAL. SYSTEM CONFIGU-RATION COMPLETE. READY FOR POLARITY TRANSFER . . .**

Tony typed on the keyboard. **SEQUENCE COMMAND ACTIVATE.**

The on-board computer blinked its response. **DESTINATION CODE ENTERED AND COORDINATED. POWER RESERVE 100 PERCENT. VOYAGER STANDING BY . . .** Tony turned to his brother. "You ready?"

Kim shifted uneasily. "You sure you know what you're doing?"

Tie Li tugged on his shirtsleeve. Kim looked down at her. "He knows," she said.

The older boy gave Tony a weak thumbs-up.

Tony turned back to the computer screen. He spoke slowly, firmly. *"Voyager, go!"*

The machine responded instantly. The workshop filled with a soft blue light, which quickly turned a brilliant white. With a sound like a strong wind, *Voyager* disappeared in a blinding flash.

Tony's invention settled on the outskirts of a small village nestled among rolling hills. After a few moments the door swung open and the boy stepped out. Tie Li followed close behind.

"How was it, Tie Li? I think the new configuration works better. It wasn't as rough as before, was it?"

"It much better," the girl agreed. "Not so many bumps."

The two stopped and looked back toward *Voyager*. "Hey, Kim," Tony called. "We're here. You can come out now."

No response.

Tie Li walked back to the doorway. She giggled. "Kim. You can open your eyes now. We here."

The older boy stepped gingerly through the entrance into the bright sunlight. He stood surveying the landscape. Flocks of sheep grazed on the lush, green grass covering the hills. Nearby, a man walked along freshly turned earth, throwing seed in a wide arc from a large cloth container slung over his shoulder.

Up the hill from where the children stood, the village rose from the fields, its streets dusty under the tread of animals and people scurrying about, busy in the business of making a living. Heavily burdened donkeys vied for position among the crowds at the market square, heading for destinations known only to the men and boys prodding them along.

Kim took in the scene with growing excitement. He watched a herd of goats make their way from the edge of town to a well buried in the hard-packed earth by a grove of tall trees.

"You did it," he whispered. Turning to Tony, he repeated the words a little louder. "Tony, you did it. We're not on the farm anymore."

"Well, we're not on *our* farm, that's for sure." Tony switched on the solar recharge unit at the base of *Voyager*.

The older boy turned to his brother. "Where are we?"

Tony looked down the hill. "Galilee. The village is called Nazareth."

Clearing his throat, Kim spoke with some uncertainty. "*When* are we?"

Tony closed the door to his machine. "About 2,000 years ago."

"Two thou—that's incredible!"

Tie Li sat down on the grass. "We only stay two hours, like before, Tony?"

"That's right, little sister. Two hours. Then we have to go back." Turning to Kim, he continued, "The people and animals can't see or hear us. We're just visiting. *Voyager's* translator circuits will allow us to hear English, no matter which language is spoken. That is, if not too many languages are spoken at the same time."

Tie Li giggled. "Like at Tower of Babel?"

Tony nodded. "That was a mess! It blew my poor overloaded system board all to pieces."

"Poof!" Tie Li threw her arms up into the air. "Some fireworks."

Kim walked a few paces toward the village, then stopped. "Why are we here? What did you want me to see?"

Tony motioned for his two companions to follow. "I'll show you. Over there lives an adopted boy just like you, Kim. His dad is a carpenter."

The children walked along the path leading up the hill. "Even though his new mom and dad take good care of him and love him, this isn't his real home. But for now he can't go back where he came from. He may never be able to go back. It depends."

Kim studied the whitewashed walls of the buildings up ahead. "Depends on what?"

"A lot of things."

The older boy was quiet for a moment. "So he has to stay here forever?"

"No. He can return to his Father's land after he does something first."

"What?" Kim stopped walking. "What does he have to do?"

Tony looked out over the peaceful pastures surrounding them. His gaze fell on the trees growing beside the well. A flock of sheep waited for their shepherd to draw water from the cool recesses below the ground. The animals waited patiently, their throats dry.

Kim walked over beside his brother. "What does he have to do, Tony? Tell me."

The boy drew in a deep breath. "He has to die. Some people will kill him."

"Who? Who will kill him?"

Tony looked first at Tie Li, then at Kim. "We will," he said.

Jeshua

WHAT do you mean, we're going to kill a boy? You're crazy! I'm not going to kill anybody!'' Kim folded his arms over his chest. "How can you say such a stupid thing?"

Tie Li joined in the protest. "I not hurt anybody. Take me back home. I don't want to stay here."

"No, wait!" Tony lifted his hands pleadingly. "You don't understand. Let me finish!"

The older boy stood glowering at Tony, his face shadowed with anger.

"The adopted son came here willingly. He knew what would happen."

Kim pointed his finger at Tony. "But you said *we* were going to kill him."

"In a way we are." Tony searched for words. "I don't mean we're going to walk up and stab him with a knife or shoot him or anything like that. We're the *reason* he's going to die."

Kim looked toward the village. "But why? Why does He have to die? I don't want that to happen to anybody. He doesn't have to die for me. I didn't ask Him to.''

Tie Li kicked at a stone. "He not have to die for me, either.''

Tony's voice softened. "I know. It seems weird to me, too. But that's the way it is.''

The three continued walking, following the path winding up the hill toward the edge of the village. Kim glanced at the sheep drinking deeply from the water being poured into the trough by the well. "Why would someone choose to come here when he knew something horrible would happen to him?''

The streets echoed with the shouts of sellers at the marketplace. Flocks of sheep, following sun-browned boys and strong men, added their bleating to the clattering of hooves on stone. Brightly colored folds of cloth hung from wooden racks. Women, wrapped in long, billowy gowns fingered the textiles and argued for bargains. Other villagers strode by, balancing large water jars on their heads, sometimes stopping to admire the wares spread on low tables beside the road.

The buildings were made of mud bricks and stone. Through opened windows and doors came the laughter and cries of children at play. The dry air carried the scent of baking bread and salted fish. Above the crowded rows of houses the bright afternoon sun sent warm rays reflecting down each dusty street.

Rounding a corner, Tony lifted his hand, motioning for the group to stop. "Over there. I think that's it.''

The three found themselves in front of a small whitewashed dwelling. Handcrafted woodworking tools rested in the doorway. Peering inside, they saw a pile of shavings and sawdust covering a corner of the room. More tools hung from wooden rafters.

Tony spoke softly. "This is where the boy lives."

Straw mats covered portions of the hard-packed dirt floor. Against a far wall an open fireplace cuddled the ashes left from the noonday meal. A low wooden table, surrounded by hard, rough wood stools, sat beside a row of large earthen jars, several filled with water. Flat loaves of bread lay stacked in one corner of the room. "Father?"

The children were startled by the sound of someone calling. They turned to see a young child hurrying down the street toward them. "Father, are you in there?"

The boy entered the house, looked around, then stepped back out into the sunshine. "Father?"

A voice answered from next door. "Jeshua, is that you?"

"Yes, I'm back. Mother said I can help you now. Are we going to make a table like we did yesterday?"

A broad, muscular man emerged from the house next door and joined his Son in front of their one-room dwelling. "That's right. You think you're up to it?"

The child nodded enthusiastically as his father led the way into the house. The boy grabbed one end of a long plank of wood by the workbench. "I want to be strong like you, Father. At the synagogue last Sabbath the rabbi said I should learn to work hard. It pleases God." The wood settled with a thud on the table. "Sometimes pleasing God makes my arms tired."

"Mine, too," the father agreed with a smile. "The rabbi is a good man. He knows the Scriptures. If he said hard work pleases God, it pleases God."

The two lifted another long board onto the workbench. The child strained under the load. "Is God always so hard to please?"

"Sometimes." The man helped ease the wood into

position, then grabbed a saw hanging overhead. "Other times it's easy to do what God wants. I suppose it depends on how much you love Him."

"I love Him." The boy said, then hesitated. "At least, I think I do. It's hard to love someone you can't see. Why doesn't God come down here and talk to us like He did to King David and Job and those other people the rabbi reads about? Then I could know what God is really like. Then I could love Him for sure."

The man stopped sawing and studied his son's face. "Not a bad idea, Jeshua. He should do that."

Nodding, the child took a firm grip on the wood, ready to hold it steady while his father sawed.

"Ouch!" The boy stepped back from the workbench, holding his outstretched hand.

The man dropped the saw and hurried over to his son. "What happened? Are you all right?"

"It hurts, Father." A splinter of wood protruded from the child's open palm. "It hurts."

The man bent low and gently removed the splinter. A small trickle of blood moistened the boy's palm. His bottom lip quivered as he fought back tears.

"There, you'll be OK, son. I fixed it for you."

Jeshua felt himself encircled by strong arms. The boy's father lifted him off the floor and held him tightly. "Does it feel better now?"

The little boy buried his face in his father's broad shoulders. He cried softly, feeling the warm love flowing from this man who meant the world to him. Whenever hurt or fear threatened, he knew the strong arms of his father waited nearby, ready to enclose him in the safe boundaries of his embrace.

Tony, Tie Li, and Kim watched in silence, each lost in

memories from their own experience. Kim hesitated, then spoke in a whisper. "My father was like that."

Tie Li reached up and took her brother's hand in hers. "I remember," she said.

A woman entered the room, a bundle of firewood over her shoulder. "What's the matter Joseph?" she asked when she saw the man and child by the workbench. "Did something happen to Jeshua?"

Joseph smiled at his wife. "Nothing a little love can't heal. I'm afraid our hard worker got poked by a piece of wood."

She wiped tears from the boy's face and added her arms to the embrace.

Joseph looked down at his wife. "Jeshua was just telling me how he wished God would come down and talk to us like he did with our ancestors."

A shadow crept across Mary's face. She took the wounded hand in hers. Seeing the trickle of blood, the woman closed her eyes tightly, as if to chase away a terrible vision.

Mary took the child from Joseph's arms and held him close, her hands forming fists behind Jeshua's back. "No," she whispered. "Not yet." She pressed the child's head against her chest. "Please. Not yet."

Kim's eyes opened wide. "She knows. Tony, she knows!"

Tony motioned for his companions to follow him away from the little house. "We have to get back to *Voyager*. Our time is up."

The three walked in silence through the narrow streets. Soon they were standing at the base of Tony's machine.

Kim looked back toward the village. "I don't understand. I'm confused by all this. Who is that little boy?

What's going to happen to him?''

Tony set the switches on the panel above his head. ''We'll find out soon enough. Come on. Let's go home.''

Voyager disappeared from view, leaving the hillside empty except for the sound of the wind and the gentle lowing of sheep. In the village, a little boy sped along a dusty street, happily running an errand for the father he loved.

A mother wept. Her first born was growing up too fast. She watched her son disappear around a corner. But the road continued south, through the marketplace, down into the Plain of Esdraelon, and over the horizon, finally ending at the cold stone walls of Jerusalem.

First Step

DR. McFERREN leaned back in his chair, a look of surprise lifting his dark eyebrows. "Do I what?" Kim cleared his throat and spoke slowly, quietly. "Do you believe in God?"

"Well, I . . ." The man drummed his fingers on the glassy surface of his desk. "Sure, I guess so. I mean, I used to, but . . ." Dr. McFerren rose to his feet. "We're not here to discuss me. I'm supposed to ask the questions. Let's not get off the track, OK?"

Kim watched the doctor brush invisible dust from the back of his large leather chair. "God is not being analyzed here. You are. I prefer we keep it that way. Now," the man returned to his seat, "where were we? Oh, yes. You were telling me about the medical doctor at the jungle clinic. Go on, please."

Kim studied Dr. McFerren's face for a moment. There was a shadow of uncertainty darkening the otherwise friendly countenance. He wasn't sure of the reason behind the doctor's sudden agitation. He'd asked a simple question. At least, he thought it was simple. The man had been taken aback by it, and Kim wondered why.

"I just wanted to know, that's all," the boy explained, shifting in his chair. "Someone told me about a God who lived many years ago and I . . ."

"Kim!" The doctor's face reddened. He looked around the room, then back at his patient. "Kim, please. God has nothing to do with us. We speak of reality in this room, not religion."

The man seemed suddenly tired. His hands grew limp in his lap. "God lives in old songs and cold, stone buildings. His name belongs on the lips of innocent children, not where men think for themselves."

"But wasn't He a man once, a human being like us?"

The doctor's jaw clenched. "If He was, He would have understood."

"Understood what?" Kim hesitated. "Dr. McFerren, what do you mean? What are you talking about?"

The man shook his head as if to clear his thoughts. "Our time is up, Kim. I'll see you next week. Mr. Parks is waiting for you in the lobby."

With that, Dr. McFerren hurriedly left the room, leaving Kim sitting alone in the big office.

Tie Li watched leafless branches rush by the bus window. The laughter of classmates blended with the whine of gears, creating a familiar, almost comfortable, background to her thoughts.

Tony sat next to her, lost in the pages of a computer magazine. Every once in a while he'd make a notation in a little notebook, then return to the article.

"Just few more days."

"What's that? What'd you say?" Tony looked down at his sister.

"I said, just few more days, then Kim will ride on bus with us."

"Yup." Tony closed the magazine and gazed out the window. "I wonder if he'll like our school."

"I wonder if our school will like *him*." The girl sighed. "It hard to go to a new school."

Tony smiled. "You and I both know about that, don't we?"

The girl nodded. "We experienced."

"Wow, Tie Li, where'd you learn such a big word?"

The girl pointed at the pile of books on her lap. "I read it in here." She sorted among them until she found a large volume Tony recognized as a dictionary. "I want to learn to speak English very outstanding."

Tony stifled a laugh. "Well, you're certainly doing a good job. I'll bet your teachers think you're really smart."

The girl straightened a stack of papers. "Mrs. Alderman says I'm learning words she never heard of."

"I'm sure she does."

"It because I'm experienced."

"I see."

The bus bounced along the country road, passing snow-covered fields and farms. Tony and Tie Li listened to the chatter coming from the seats around them. Would Kim learn to feel at home here? Or would the laughter be aimed at him? Time would tell.

That night at the dinner table, Mr. Parks reported he had some very exciting news. It concerned Grandmother.

Tie Li put down her soup spoon and looked across at her father. News from Grandmother was about the only thing capable of making the little girl stop eating.

Mr. Parks cleared his throat and began. "As you all

know, my mother has been ill for some time, but the doctors say she's getting better.

"I don't want her to live by herself in the city anymore, so I've asked her to come live with us, if that's OK with all of you."

Tie Li's eyes opened wide. "She coming here to live? Here on farm?"

"Well, sort of," the man continued. "I thought we could fix up the cabin for her. That way, she'd have her independence, and we'd be nearby to keep an eye on her."

Tie Li almost rose off the chair. "When she come? When she come?"

Mr. Parks looked at Tony. "What do you think son? Can we take care of her all right?"

A big smile spread across the boy's face. "I think it's a great idea, Dad. We insulated the cabin last fall. I can install a phone for her and stuff like that."

"And how about you, Kim?" Mr. Parks looked over at the older boy. "Will you help us too?"

Tie Li waited for her brother's answer. She had never seen him respond in any way to either Mr. or Mrs. Parks when it came to family affairs. The girl's breath caught in her throat.

Kim pushed his spoon through his soup without looking up. Then he spoke quietly. "I'll help."

Mrs. Parks slipped her hand over her husband's. He felt her grip tighten. She looked at the boy sitting at the far end of the table. "Thank you, Kim," she said, almost in a whisper.

Tie Li closed her eyes. A turning point had been reached. It may have been just a small step, but long journeys begin with small steps. In silence she picked up her spoon and began eating again. How good the food tasted!

For the next couple days the cabin fell under the attack of hardworking, eager hands. Each afternoon after school, Tony and Tie Li joined the rest of the family in the little clearing, making sure all was ready for the important new tenant.

Floors were scrubbed, windows cleaned, dishes washed and neatly stacked in freshly papered cupboards. Bedding was brought from the big yellow house along with cooking utensils. Dad installed a new refrigerator and stove, and Tony filled the bookcases with old favorites. Grandmother loved to read, so he made sure the most exciting adventure story books found their way onto her shelves. Tie Li understood. Both she and Tony loved to be read too.

True to his word, Kim worked alongside the rest of the family. Though he seldom spoke, they were satisfied just to have him there. Dr. McFerren had said Kim could return to school soon. He encouraged involvement with others, as this would make the transition to the world beyond the farm easier.

"How's this look?" Mrs. Parks held a picture up against the wall. "Do you think it goes with this room?"

Tie Li glanced up from her cleaning, studied the picture, and nodded. "It extraordinary."

Mrs. Parks blinked. She looked over at Tony. He shrugged.

"Well, thank you, Tie Li," Mother said, reaching for a nail. "I'm glad you approve."

The girl continued her scrubbing.

The big day arrived. Mr. Parks left early for the long drive to the city. The rest of the family stayed behind, adding last minute touches to the cabin. A colorful bouquet of flowers bloomed in the vase centered on the kitchen table.

Tony tested the phone system while his brother stacked wood in the large fireplace. As Kim watched Tony check the wiring on the wall phone, he remembered the night they'd spent sitting in front of the cabin's warm fire several weeks before. That was the night Tony had told him about a God who had become a man. And later he'd taken him in *Voyager* to the little town on the dusty hillside. Everything was so new and confusing. Even Dr. McFerren wouldn't give him a straight answer about this strange God-man.

The boy sighed. In his mind, he could see his old home beside the jungle, his father bending in the hot sun, harvesting rice plants. If only he could talk to his father again. He'd know what to do. He'd have the answers.

"We're here!" The front door of the cabin burst open as Mr. Parks entered the room. Behind him stood Grandmother wrapped in brightly colored scarves, her hat pulled low over her face to keep out the brisk winter air.

"Grandmother!" Tie Li ran across the room and threw herself into waiting arms.

Tony placed the phone on its cradle and stood in line for his hug.

Mrs. Parks took the woman's coat and hung it on a hook by the door. "We're glad to see you, Mother Parks," she said warmly. "Welcome to your new home."

Grandmother smiled at her family and looked about the room. "How lovely you've made everything! It's—it's—"

"Monumental?" Tie Li encouraged.

Grandmother drew in a breath. "Why, that's exactly the word I was searching for. It's monumental."

Tie Li beamed up at Tony. Her lips moved silently. "Experience."

Tony winked and nodded. "Very experienced."

"And this must be Kim." Grandmother walked across the room, her hand outstretched. "How do you do, Kim? I'm glad to meet you."

The boy slowly reached out his hand. Grandmother held his gaze with hers. "I've heard a lot about you. I think we're going to be good friends."

Kim looked into the eyes that were soft with understanding, filled with wonderful secrets.

"Yes, I'd like that," he said.

Another Name

THE electric heater resting in the corner of Tony's workshop hummed softly. Words and symbols flickered on and off the computer screen as the little red light on the disk drive responded to the rhythmic tapping of his fingers on the keys.

"There," Tony said, studying the amber glow before him. "Just one more entry and we can go."

Tie Li and Kim sat nearby, watching their brother. Kim was beginning to admire Tony's attention to detail in all that he did. Even the workshop reflected his passion for organization. Everything had an assigned place. If only life could be so ordered.

Tie Li's chin rested on her fist, her elbow pressing against the tabletop. She watched Tony's fingers fly across the keyboard. Every once in a while she would glance over at Kim. Even now it was hard to believe he was alive and well, sitting in this room with her. How lucky she felt, and how very happy! She knew Kim loved her very much. There was just too much hurt inside him. He'd get better someday. He had to.

"Where are we going this time?" Kim's voice broke the sleepy stillness of the room. "Will we see the little boy again?"

Tony straightened in his chair and rubbed the back of his neck. "Well, sort of. The little boy won't be so little anymore. He's 12 years old. He and his family haven't moved away from Nazareth though. You guys ready to go?"

The children walked over to Tony's machine and settled in their assigned places. "This still makes me nervous," Kim muttered as he helped Tie Li slip on her football helmet.

"Me too," Tony agreed, pressing in close to his passengers.

"What?" Kim looked up in surprise.

"Just kidding, big brother," Tony laughed. "You'll be all right. Haven't lost anybody yet."

Tie Li snickered. "Just so it doesn't rain."

Kim cleared his throat. "What's she mean by that?"

"Don't mind her." Tony looked down at his sister. "We had a little problem once, but we made it back all right. *Voyager's* a good, solid machine, but it doesn't like rain very much."

"Is it raining where we're going?" Kim persisted.

"Nah, it doesn't rain much there. We'll be OK."

Kim didn't seem convinced as Tony closed the door. After making some adjustments and setting some dials, the boy spoke in the darkness. *"Voyager,* power up!"

As before, lights and screens flickered to life, responding to Tony's voice and keyboard commands. Soon the workshop glowed with a familiar blue light that quickly turned a brilliant white. In a flash, *Voyager* disappeared. Before long the children felt the big, wooden box settle with a dull thud. Tony busied himself putting the machine's internal systems on standby and resetting the countdown timer.

Reaching up to adjust the stabilizer arm control, Tony felt something splash on the back of his hand.

"What's this?" Tony opened the door to let some light in. He closed it again quickly.

"Tony, can we go out now?" Tie Li tried to shift her weight in the cramped quarters.

"Well, no, not just yet."

Suddenly Kim called out. "Hey, something just dropped on my head. It feels like—like—"

"Water," Tony interrupted. "It's water. I believe it's raining outside."

"What?" Kim fairly shouted. "It's raining? You said—"

"I know. I said it doesn't rain *much* here."

"What we do now?" Tie Li sounded concerned.

"Follow me." Tony opened the door and stepped out into the downpour. His companions trailed behind as he made his way to the rear of the machine. From the back of an access panel, he pulled out a large plastic sheet folded into a tight square. The children hurriedly spread it out on the wet grass, then with Tie Li perched on Kim's shoulders, they slipped the cover over the top of *Voyager,* shielding it from the rain. Then the three jumped back inside Tony's invention.

After their huffing and puffing subsided, Kim spoke in the darkness. "Tony, I want you to know something."

Tony looked over at his brother.

"I want you to know that I appreciate how good you take care of my . . . of our little sister. I just want you to know that."

The rain drummed on *Voyager's* makeshift cover, creating a staccato sound. The younger boy nodded slowly. "It's OK, Kim. I enjoy watching out for her." Tony hesitated, then continued. "But sometimes I could use a little help."

Kim pulled dark, wet hair from his eyes. He rested his head against a panel of switches. "I . . . I'd like to help. I just don't know how anymore."

The boy felt a tiny hand slip into his. A small voice drifted in the damp darkness. "You know how, Kim. Remember in our village? You always walk with me when I went to see Father in the fields. Sometimes you carry me. And I was scared of the big dog, and you chase it away. You a very good brother, like Tony. I want you to take care of me because I love you."

Kim's hand tightened around Tie Li's. "I miss our village. I miss Mother and Father very much." He turned then, speaking almost fiercely. "Will the pain ever go away?"

The girl pressed her moist face against her brother's arm. "It not go away; it change. Now when I think of our village, of Mother and Father, the pain make me smile. And when I hear your voice, I smile and there is no pain. You can learn to smile when you think of before. You can learn how, just like me."

The steady drum of the rain slowly softened into silence. Tony stood in the quiet confines of his machine, not wanting to break the serenity of the moment. His heart was singing. He knew how much Kim's words meant to Tie Li. "I think the rain has stopped." Tony pushed open the door and stuck his head out into the cool, fresh air. "Yup. We can go now. We'd better hurry."

The three made their way along the muddy path leading

toward the village. Before they had gone far, they noticed a woman and a boy walking toward them. "Wait," Tony called. "That's them! We need to follow."

The trio fell in behind the couple heading up the hill, away from the village. The two walked in silence, the boy helping His mother over some rough places in the path. Soon they crested the hill and sat down on a large rock to rest. Tony, Tie Li, and Kim sat nearby, waiting to see what was going to happen.

"But Mother," the boy was saying, "I don't understand. All the other boys my age have been attending the rabbi's school for years. I see them pass by our house every morning. When can I go too? They make fun of me. They say I must be sick or feebleminded or some such thing."

"Are you?"

"Don't you make fun of me too!"

"I'm sorry." The woman placed her hand on her son's shoulder. "I know it's been hard on you, not being allowed to attend classes with the rest. I've taught you for the past six years because I wanted to make sure you learned all the things that are important. I wanted you to know about the God of heaven, about nature, about the flowers and trees, and about people—why they act the way they do. I wanted you to be prepared for what lies ahead." A shadow darkened the woman's face. "You must be prepared. It's important that you know the truth."

"Mother, you look so serious. What truth should I know about?"

The woman drew in a deep breath. "Jeshua, you are a very special young man. Very special. And someday . . ." Her voice faltered. "Someday . . . You'll have a special work to do."

"I know." The boy spoke confidently. "I'm to be a carpenter like Father."

"No, you will not be a carpenter."

The boy looked up in surprise. "I must be a carpenter. Father is training me."

The woman stood to her feet and walked a few paces away from the rock. She spoke slowly, carefully selecting each word. "Before you were born, an angel came to me and said I was to have a son, and that . . ." she hesitated, trying to control her emotions, ". . . and that he would have a certain work to do. The angel even gave you a name."

"My name is Jeshua."

The woman smiled at her Son. "Yes, that's your Hebrew name. But you have another."

The boy stood and joined his mother. "I have another name? What is it? Mother, what is my name?"

"Your name . . . Your name is Immanuel."

The boy searched his mother's face. "What does that mean, Mother? What does Immanuel mean?"

Tears began to flow down the woman's cheeks. She threw her arms around her son's neck and wept, her sobs coming from deep within her. It was as if she were saying goodbye to him, as if he were leaving on a long journey.

Slowly she lifted her hands to the boy's face and gently stroked his hair. For a long moment she looked into his eyes. Then, in a whisper, she spoke. "It means . . . God with us."

Choices

THE boy stood motionless, soundlessly repeating the words his mother had just spoken. "God with us. God with us."

Turning to the woman he whispered, "But Mother, that name should be given to the Promised One, the Saviour foretold by the prophets."

The woman lifted her hand and stroked the boy's head. "It has been, my son."

Realization crept across the child's face. "Me?" he asked breathlessly. "I am the Promised One?"

His mother nodded. "You are the Son of God, the Saviour of mankind."

Kim stood to his feet. "The Son of God is just a boy? He's not any older than I am!" He looked over at Tony. "I'm supposed to believe that this kid became the great man I've heard you talk about? He didn't even go to school like everybody else! Look at him. He's just . . . just a kid!"

Tony spread his hands apart in a gesture of helplessness. "Hey, I don't make this stuff up. You're looking at reality, something that really happened."

The boy turned to his mother. "Wait. If I am Jesus, the one the prophet Isaiah called the Lamb, then—" His voice caught in His throat. "Then I must—"

"Jeshua, I didn't mean for this to happen. It was not my wish. But God has placed you in this world for the purpose of saving a lost people. You are His Son as much as you are mine. No one else can claim such a miracle.

"You have been given a very important work to do. But first, you must learn to know your Heavenly Father. That's what I've been preparing you for. When you believe in Him with all your heart, He will guide you and be with you, no matter what happens."

"But, Mother," the boy protested, "I don't want to be the Lamb. Don't you remember what Isaiah said would happen to Him?"

The woman closed her eyes as she spoke. "You are the Son of God. He will stand by you. And I . . . I will always love you."

Jeshua pressed close to his mother. "I am frightened. I don't want to be God's Son."

The woman lovingly stroked his hair. "It's not a choice you can make. You *are* the Promised One." She looked into her son's face. "But how you live your life is up to You. You can turn your back on your Heavenly Father and your mission. You can choose not to follow what you know to be your purpose in life. It's up to you, my son. There will be no one to take your place."

Tony spoke, his words almost a whisper. "It's too much to ask of a young boy. If he says yes, he will someday fulfill the prophecy. If he says no, sin will rule the world forever."

"What prophecy?" Kim asked. "What does the prophecy say?"

"It says the Lamb of God will be slaughtered."

Tie Li walked toward the couple, her eyes not leaving the face of the boy. "I'm sorry," she said, even though she knew no one heard. "I'm sorry you have to do this. I understand if you say no. I understand if you run away and hide."

A signal sounded from Tony's watch. "Our time is up," he reported. "We have to get back to *Voyager*."

Kim hesitated. "But what's the kid going to do?"

"We'll have to find out later. Come on," Tony urged. "Let's go!"

The three made their way back down the hill. Kim walked in silence until they reached the machine. "It's not fair to ask a kid to be something he doesn't want to be. I mean, who would choose to end up being a sacrifice? I know I wouldn't."

"I know I wouldn't, either," Tony agreed, pulling the plastic cover off his invention. "But there's more to it than what we see. It's the same with us, I guess. Our decisions affect more than just ourselves. Sometimes we have to do something we don't want to do because it will help someone else. True, it's not fair. It just is."

Kim looked back up the hill. "I don't know. When you told me about Creation back at the cabin, I could believe that because it explained a lot of stuff I wondered about. The serpent, sin, evil—I can believe that, too. But this . . ." The boy pointed toward the crest of the hill. "How can a kid be the Son of God? He's just . . . a kid like us!"

Tony entered the machine and motioned for the others to follow. "I guess we'll find out later." As an afterthought he added, "Maybe we kids can do more than we think we can."

Soon, *Voyager* flashed white and disappeared, leaving

the pasture empty and still. On the crest of the hill, two figures stood silhouetted against the sky. The world waited for a Saviour.

* * *

Kim awoke with a start. Someone was knocking on his door. Rubbing his eyes, he sat up and peered into the darkness. "Who is it?" he called, his voice rough from slumber.

"It me, Tie Li."

"What do you want?"

Tie Li opened the door and stuck her head into the room. "It's time for you to get up. Today you go to new school."

Kim blinked, trying to ward off the bright light shining through the open door. "But it's still night," he protested. "Come back when the sun's up." He fell back against his pillow.

Tie Li opened the door wider and entered the room. "It not night. It school morning. The sun never gets up before us. It must be sleepyhead like you."

Kim mumbled and turned over, covering his head with a blanket. Tie Li continued her attack. "It is time to rise and glow. Don't you smell breakfast cooking? We going to have eggs and pancakes with good stuff on top. You like pancakes?"

"Go away."

"Don't you want to go to school? They have nice teachers, fun games at recess, and really cute girls."

Kim stirred. "Girls? What girls?"

"Tony told me to say that."

Kim pulled the covers from his face. "What do you know about boys and girls?"

"I know everything."

"Everything?"

57

"I know boys don't like girls and girls don't like boys."

"Smart girl."

Tie Li turned to leave. "Come on, Kim. Get up now. I'll sit beside you on bus if you want."

"But I'm a boy," Kim yawned. "What will everyone say?"

"You not a boy. You my brother. Now, *get up!*"

Tie Li slipped out of the room and ran down the attic stairs. Kim lay in bed listening to her footsteps as she skipped the length of the hall and stopped at Tony's door. "Come on, Tony," he heard her say. "If you don't hurry, I will eat all your pancakes."

Kim slowly sat up in bed. How cheerful his sister's voice sounded. It was one of the things he had missed most when he thought she was . . .

He shook his head and yawned again. The covers felt so warm, the world so cold. Pulling back the curtains hanging over the window by his bed, he peered into the darkness. A faint blush of morning tinged the eastern sky. The trees beyond the pasture stood stark and foreboding, like sentinels waiting to defend the night against the creeping approach of day.

Kim rested his chin on the sill. School. What would it be like in this strange land? He had always enjoyed his studies. The government-operated learning centers had not been the most modern in the world, but the teachers always encouraged him to work hard, especially in English class. "Language of tomorrow" they called it. He found mastering this strange dialect challenging, but rewarding. It seemed that "tomorrow" had arrived.

The boy slipped out of bed and fumbled for his robe. Shivering, he slowly made his way down the attic stairs and headed for the bathroom. Maybe a hot shower would wake him up.

"Good morning!" Tony's voice carried through the open door of his bedroom. "I see you've been 'Tie Li'ed' too."

Kim nodded. It seemed his sister served a dual purpose in the Parks' estate. She disposed of most of the food, especially chocolate-chip cookies, and also provided regular wake-up service to the occupants of the big yellow house.

As the warm water splashed over his face, Kim let his mind drift back to the hilltop outside Nazareth. He thought of the Boy and His mother, of the choices He faced.

Why were there always decisions to be made? Why couldn't life be simple? Then, he thought of Tie Li. She depended on the decisions other people made. All children did. Everything that happened to her, good or bad, was the result of someone, or some government making a choice, a decision. The enemy soldiers, the commanding officers, Sister Martinez, Mr. and Mrs. Parks, Tony, all had made decisions for or against Tie Li. And she had to live with the results of those choices.

Kim lathered shampoo into his hair. What power there was in making choices—what tremendous power.

The family had already started eating when Kim entered the kitchen. "Here are your pancakes," Tie Li called. "I saved them for you."

Kim took his place at the table. Mrs. Parks spooned a steaming pile of scrambled eggs onto his dish and poured creamy white milk into his glass.

The boy looked about the table. Warm smiles and happy talk filtered through the kitchen along with the smell of fresh bread. He listened for a while, then suddenly stood to his feet. All talking stopped.

Walking around the table, Kim knelt beside Tie Li's chair, put his arms around his sister, and gave her a long, gentle hug.

Tie Li was taken by surprise. "Why, Kim? Why you give me such a nice hug?"

Kim looked into her eyes and smiled. "I don't know," he said. "Just something I chose to do."

He returned to his chair, and began eating breakfast. He felt happy inside—happier than he'd been for a long, long time.

Face in the Crowd

THE rattling, noisy school bus ground to a halt on the cold, windswept country road. Tony, Tie Li, and Kim clamored aboard and began searching for seats among the chattering children lining the long aisle running the length of the vehicle.

Tie Li seemed to be walking a few inches off the ground. What other girl in school had the honor of being escorted by two big brothers? She figured she must be the luckiest person in the entire world.

Kim found a place near the back and, as promised, Tie Li squeezed in beside him. The only seat left for Tony was several rows forward. He started to sit down, but suddenly realized the bundled body waiting next to the window, right beside where he had to sit, was a *girl!*

"Hi, Tony." A soft voice spoke from under the red scarf wrapped around the young traveler's mouth. Dark curls protruded from under her colorful cap, framing a pair of big brown eyes.

Tony looked up and down the isle, searching in vain for another empty seat, but none was available. "Hi," he said nervously, resigning himself to the fact that his worst fears were coming true. He'd have to sit next to a girl all the way to school.

The boy settled into his place, keeping as far away from the form by the window as possible. He placed his lunch pail, gloves, cap, books, notepad—anything he could find—between him and the girl. Tony didn't mind computers, test tubes, cows, chickens, old people, and winter storms. But girls weren't high on his list of things he wanted to keep company with, to say nothing of sit next to.

The girl ignored Tony's attempts at segregation. "You ready for today's algebra test?" she asked. Then waving her hand in the air she quickly added, "Oh, that's right. You always get A's in school. I wish I was smart like you."

Tony glanced at the girl, then out the window. "What makes you think I get all A's in school? You don't even know me."

"Yes, I do," the girl responded, encouraged by Tony's weak acknowledgment of her existence. "I sit two rows behind you in home class. I'm Laura. Laura Bates. Last week you knocked my eraser off my desk. You picked it up and said 'I'm sorry' and everything. You're a real gentleman."

Tony squirmed. "No, I don't remember. I've got to do some reading." He picked up a book and leafed through the pages, then settled into silence.

After a few moments, the girl tapped him on the arm.

"What?" he said without looking up.

"How do you do that?" Laura bent over the pile between them, her cap nearly touching his cheek.

"Do what?" Tony responded, leaning away from her.

"That," she said, pointing at the open book. "How can you read up-side-down? Isn't it harder that way?"

62

Tony felt his face burn with embarrassment. He flipped the book over. "I . . . I was just studying the pictures. I wanted to see what they looked like from a different angle."

"Oh." The girl sat back in her seat. "That makes sense, I guess. I'll have to try it sometime."

Tony closed his eyes in frustration. *That was stupid,* he thought to himself. *Why in the world was I looking at my book up-side-down? I think I'm losing my mind.*

He glanced at the girl. She was watching the snowy landscape speed by beyond the frost-framed window. *It's all her fault,* he concluded. *She made me get confused or something. Women. They're weird.*

He looked at the book in his lap, then closed his eyes again. It was one of Tie Li's. Worst of all, it was her second grade grammar book. The picture he had been so intently studying showed a dinosaur and elephant talking together under a large palm tree. Tony wished a big hole would open up and swallow him then and there.

A few rows back, Tie Li sat proudly next to her older brother, hoping everyone would notice how handsome he looked in his new coat and cap.

"You will like this school," she said for the twentieth time. "The teachers are very nice, and they play fun games at recess, and you get a big locker in the hallway, and you can listen to records in the library, and—"

"I know," Kim smiled. "Someone already told me all about it."

Tie Li grinned up at him. She let out a contented sigh. "You will like this school."

The day moved slowly, as some days do. Kim reported to the registrar's office, filled in and signed numerous forms, talked with several counselors, took a short test, took a long test, ate lunch with Tie Li and Tony, took another test, was assigned a locker, gathered an armload of books, and finally, with more than enough fanfare, was left standing before dozens of staring eyes in Mr. Parson's 8th-grade classroom.

"We're glad to have you with us," the smiling teacher encouraged after introductions were over. "Your seat is over there, by the window. We're just beginning our history lesson for the day. We'll give you time to settle in before we continue."

All eyes followed the new student as he made his way toward the empty desk by the window. If only someone would say something to break the awful silence. Kim shuffled along, his load of books and papers making him feel awkward, uncoordinated.

Suddenly, his foot caught on something. He felt himself falling forward, unable to stop. He saw the edge of his desk coming straight for his face, but there was no time to protect himself.

He hit hard, the shock sending bright flashes of light arching across his vision. Then, it seemed he was falling a great distance, from some high pinnacle. He saw his books floating by, his papers and pencils spinning in space just beyond reach. With a final bone-jarring crash, he sprawled across the floor, hot searing pain shooting from the right side of his face and running down the entire length of his body.

He fought for consciousness. Waves of nausea swept over him like an ocean tide. A bodyless face appeared close to his, its eyes narrow, cold. It was speaking to him in a hoarse whisper. "My uncle was killed by one of you slant-eyed monsters. You just watch yourself. You hear me, monster? You just watch your step."

The face seemed to swim in a darkening sky, then all went black. Kim felt as if he were floating in space, like he wasn't attached to anything. He could hear voices, but they seemed far away. Echoes drifted through his mind. Formless shadows moved in and out of a revolving universe of black and gray. Then all was quiet, still, motionless.

"Kim?" A gentle voice called from somewhere in the silence. "Kim, can you hear me?"

The boy tried to move, but pain kept him rigid.

"Kim, I'm Nurse Anderson. Can you hear me?"

Light began to seep in around the corners of his vision. He saw a fuzzy form bending over him, speaking his name over and over again.

Another voice joined the first. This one he recognized. "Kim, Kim! Wake up. You wake up now." The voice began to cry. "Please Kim. Please, wake up now."

It was Tie Li. He tried to smile, but the pain forced him to give up the effort. He opened his eyes a little farther. A woman wearing a white cap looked down at him. Sudden relief showed on her face. "He's coming around. Look, he's awake."

"What . . . happened?" Kim spoke through the throbbing ache in his swollen jaw.

Tony stepped up beside the bed. "Somebody tripped you. You were on your way to your desk and some idiot tripped you."

Kim began to remember. Yes. He was trying to get to his seat as soon as he could. Then he fell. He saw the edge of the desk coming toward him. He couldn't stop. He couldn't . . .

Kim stiffened as Tony's words sunk in. Someone had tripped him. Somebody in that room had stuck out his foot and tripped him.

Kim sat up, the pain nearly knocking him off the examining table. He grabbed Tony's arm, and in one move, landed on the floor, his legs nearly buckling under the strain. He staggered toward the door, the screams of Tie Li and the nurse grinding in his ears like fingernails on a blackboard.

The hallway was almost empty. Most of the students were out by the buses, waiting to board.

Kim staggered to the front door and kicked it open with his foot. The glass shattered as the door struck the outside wall. Students scattered in all directions as Kim emerged from the building and stopped at the top of the stairs.

Silence gripped the assembly. No one moved. All eyes were on the boy with the discolored, swollen face standing at the entrance to the building. Kim searched the sea of faces, fighting to keep his vision clear, and to remain on his feet.

"I know you're out there," he called, steadying himself against the stabbing pain punctuating each word. "I know what you look like. We will meet again. If you want to keep a war alive that ended years ago, that can be arranged. But know this." Kim's finger swept the crowd. "Wars are deadly for both sides. Your battle is coming. It always does."

Kim turned and stumbled back into the building. Slowly, the faces in the crowd melted into activity once again as students continued their afterschool routine. All, that is, except one. This face remained motionless, staring at the place where Kim had stood. It's eyes grew narrow. It's lips formed a thin, tight line. Below, knuckles turned white inside gloved fists. For the mind behind the face, Kim's words rang true. The war was far from over.

Warrior

WHAT on earth happened to you?'' Grandmother Parks gasped as Kim and the others entered her cabin that night. ''Are you all right?''

Tony threw his coat over the hook by the door. ''Some eighth grader decided Kim was too handsome, so he tried to rearrange his face a little.''

''Somebody hit him with a desk,'' Tie Li added, warming her hands by the fire. ''Not a very nice thing to do.''

''That's for sure,'' Grandmother agreed, running to the kitchen to turn up the fire under the teakettle. ''I'll fix a hot cloth to put on it. Should help the swelling go down. Desks can be very hard on faces.''

''You can say that again,'' Kim groaned, easing into a chair by the kitchen table. ''Lucky my head is hard. At least that's what the doctor said.''

Grandmother sighed. ''Some people can be very cruel, can't they? It's hard to love them when they're like that.''

''Love them?'' Kim looked up in surprise. ''What do you mean love them?''

The woman gently placed a steaming, wet cloth over the swollen jaw. "Maybe love's not the right word. How about . . . forgive? Yes, that's much better. Not quite so emotional."

"I'm supposed to forgive that jerk? No way! If he wants a war, I'll give it to him."

Grandmother Parks frowned. "It seems he already has a war. You'd just be joining it. Are you sure you want to do that?"

Kim didn't answer. The woman inspected the boy's jaw as she spoke. "For most people who fight wars, their battles don't begin on some beachhead or mountain pass. They begin in here." She pressed her hand against her chest. "A lot of people have been hurt because someone has a battle raging inside his heart."

Tony threw a piece of wood on the fire. "You mean we're supposed to let idiots like that hurt people and not do anything about it?"

"No," Grandmother countered. "We're supposed to fight them, but not in the way you think. One of the greatest warriors who ever lived never hurt anybody, yet he defeated a terrible enemy."

Tie Li sat down beside her older brother. "Who's that?" she asked. "What great warrior fights and doesn't hurt anybody?"

Grandmother returned to the sink to add more hot water to Kim's cloth. "You've seen him with your own eyes." When Kim looked surprised she added, "I know all about *Voyager*. Tony told me some time ago."

Tony nodded. "You mean the boy in Nazareth?"

Kim laughed quietly. "He's just a kid. He's no great warrior. I'll bet he couldn't win a fair fight if his life depended on it."

"Oh, but it does!" Grandmother sat down next to him. "His life, your life. He's about to face the most terrible battle in the history of the world."

"This I've got to see," Kim sneered. "That kid against the world's worst? It'll be a slaughter . . ." The word caught in Kim's throat.

"You're right," Grandmother said slowly. "That's exactly what it will be."

Kim studied the design on the tablecloth. He thought of the boy standing on the crest of the hill with his mother. Was he to fight a great battle? Some warrior. He hadn't even decided whether he wanted to accept being the Son of God.

Tony read the older boy's thoughts. "We can go tomorrow. We'll find out what happened."

Kim looked over at his brother and nodded. "Yes. I want to know."

* * *

The streets were jammed with donkeys, camels, carts, and people, all in a hurry. Colorful costumes fluttered in the warm wind as their wearers jostled for position along the smooth stone thoroughfare.

Voices called, animals protested, children laughed, vendors hawked their wares, and trumpets blared from somewhere beyond the surging flow of humanity.

"What did you call this place?" Kim maneuvered around stalls of brightly tinted cloth and rows of earthen pots. "It looks like a marketplace gone mad."

Tony chuckled, dodging a couple donkeys and trying not to lose his grip on Tie Li's hand. "Jerusalem," he called back to his companion, "the capital of Palestine."

The trio rounded a corner and stopped in their tracks. Before them was a wide-open area, crammed with people of all descriptions. Colorful booths lined the expanse. In each one they could see cages filled with birds and small animals. The bleating of sheep, mooing of cows, and incessant braying of donkeys vied for attention above the lively debate of sellers and buyers, searching for the best deal. Beyond the mix of activity and sound rose a huge stone wall, its summit stretching into the deep blue of the sky.

"Wow," Kim said breathlessly. "What a beautiful . . . uh . . . what exactly is it?"

Tony moved out into the busy arena. "It's a temple, built by a guy named Herod the Great. He used to be the Roman ruler for these parts. He wanted to impress the world with his political power, as well as keep his Jewish subjects happy, so he built it. Crowds of people come here once a year to worship during the Passover. That's what's going on now."

"Why they here?" Tie Li eyed the helmeted soldiers stationed around the compound. "Aren't these God's people? The ones we saw at Jericho?"

"Well, their great-great-great-grandchildren."

"But they are supposed to have their own country."

"They did for a while." Tony looked down at his sister. "Then they stopped obeying God, so the Romans took over. It's a long story."

The three continued across the open area and climbed the broad marble stairs leading to one of the large framed openings in the mammoth wall. They paraded through the cool dark shade under the ramparts and emerged onto another open area. It too was jammed with people.

"Court of the Gentiles," Tony said, sweeping the air with his hand. "And that," he pointed in the direction of a structure resting in the center of the compound, "is the sanctuary itself."

Tie Li caught her breath. "Oh, Tony, it's beautiful!"

White marble walls covered with shimmering plates of gold rose from massive foundations. The building was accented with golden spires that soared above the roof, sweeping the sky with their gleaming fingers. Beyond the large porch encircling the majestic structure stood immense gilded doors, covered with blue, red, and gold tapestry.

The whole building seemed to sparkle, like a jewel held up to the light. When the sun emerged from behind a passing cloud, the structure shone with almost unbearable brilliance.

The children walked toward the sanctuary, their eyes drinking in its power and radiance. "Fantastic," Kim whispered. "This has got to be the most beautiful building the world has ever seen."

A sign above the porch proclaimed in big letters, *"No foreigner allowed beyond this point. Whoever is caught will be put to death."*

"Only Jews can go in there," Tony warned. "They're very strict about that, as you can see."

The trio made their way along the outer boundary of the porch. Rounding a corner, they noticed a small group of white-robed men standing off to one side, engaged in a heated discussion. Moving closer, the children began to hear their excited conversation carrying above the noise and confusion of the crowded court.

"How can you say that?" one voice called out. "God demands obedience to His law. We are not to question. We must obey with humility and dignity."

Another speaker joined in. "Are you saying God's laws can be changed?" A startled cry rose from the gathered attendants. "I say no! We must follow the words of Scripture to the letter. It is our duty."

Yet another voice sounded from the huddle of men. "Wait! Wait! Let the lad speak. I believe his words have substance."

The men fell silent. The noise and activity surrounding the little group was ignored as all eyes studied a young boy standing in their midst.

Tie Li pointed toward the gathering. "There he is! That's the boy from Nazareth."

The children moved closer, straining to see and hear what was taking place.

"I am not saying obedience to God is unnecessary," a clear, youthful voice rang out from amid the circle of men. "I am only saying we must remember the *reasons* God created His laws in the first place. Blind obedience serves no one. But obedience out of reverence and love for the Law-giver is valuable both to God and to man."

Bearded heads nodded thoughtfully.

The boy continued, his words firm yet respectful. "We Jews worship God every week on His holy Sabbath. We bring sacrifices, pray, read from the scrolls. But are we getting so concerned about the rules governing the *way* we worship that we're losing sight of the *reason* for our homage? Worship should be the result of a thankful heart. It should not simply fulfill some list of do's and don'ts. God wants our praise as well as our obedience."

Suddenly a couple ran up to the small group of elders. "There you are!" the woman cried out. "We've been looking everywhere for you."

The children immediately recognized the boy's parents. They seemed upset, excited.

"Son," the man was saying, "we left three days ago,

72

thinking you were with others in the caravan. Outside Jericho, we discovered you weren't with us. We hurried back and have been searching for you all this time.''

The boy's mother wrapped her arms around him. ''Why? Why didn't you come to find us when you knew it was time to leave? We have worried so much. You should have let us know you wanted to stay longer. Why didn't you let us know?''

The boy looked at his mother and father. In his eyes they saw a great longing, an almost visible pain. Then they saw him search the faces of the men surrounding him. His gaze fell on the multitudes mingling in the Court of the Gentiles. A sadness crept into his young countenance.

Turning back to his mother and father, he said, ''Why did you search for me? Didn't you want me to be about my Father's business?''

The couple stared at their son. ''What do you mean by that?'' the man demanded. ''My business is in Nazareth, not here.''

''Wait.'' The woman knelt beside her young son. Placing her hands on his face, she looked deep into his eyes. ''Son, are you sure?''

The boy nodded slowly, his hands pressing against hers. ''I am sure.''

One of the elders approached the kneeling woman. ''I must say, your son is quite amazing. He speaks with great wisdom of things spiritual. He has received good training. I am certain we will be hearing from him in the years to come. Tell me, what is his name? I want to be watching for him.''

The woman rose to her feet and turned to face the elder. She spoke softly, her voice almost lost in the tumult surrounding the sanctuary. ''His name . . . is Jesus.''

Why He Came

TONY carefully placed another log on the fire and watched bright-yellow flames embrace and blacken the rough bark. He listened to the crackle and snap of burning wood and inhaled the rich, damp smell rising with the heat from the hearth.

Holding his hands in front of him, he felt a warm glow pressing against his fingers as the log ignited into a blaze of dancing, flickering flames.

"Does he really know what he's getting into?" he asked, settling himself into the big beanbag resting beside Grandmother's rocker. "Saying you're God's son is one thing. But *living* it is a different matter all together."

The boy turned and looked up into the kind face of the one sitting beside him. "He seemed a little scared, Grandma. It was sort of like he wanted to be God's son, but he was frightened at the same time. I guess I don't blame him."

The woman nodded as she rocked back and forth, her eyes not leaving the fire. "There are two kinds of Christians in this world, Tony," she said softly. "Those who say they believe in God, and those who live like they do. It takes a certain brand of determination, a special type of person, to live a life based on a belief in God. It's never easy.''

Tony sighed. ''You'd think it would be. I mean, isn't God stronger than the devil? And why is it so hard to obey what God says? I think about Adam and Eve, those workers who built the Tower of Babel, the people at the base of Noah's ark when the floods came, the children of Israel —why didn't they do what God said to do? It sure would have saved a whole bunch of problems.''

''God is stronger than the devil,'' Grandmother urged. ''But man isn't. He's weak, frail, filled with pride—all the result of sin.'' The woman looked down at her grandson. ''But not everybody has given up trying to do things God's way. Remember Noah, Moses, Joshua, Elijah, and now Mary, Jesus' mother? They didn't give up. Come what may, they did what they knew in their hearts to be right.''

Tony thought for a moment. He could see Noah standing on the battered bow of his boat, ordering his sons to build an altar to the Lord. There was Moses lifting his shepherd's rod high above the Red Sea, and Joshua leading his army around and around Jericho.

He remembered Elijah bringing the widow's son back to life, and Mary, holding her little boy tightly in her arms, tears streaming down her face as she told him of his true heritage.

Then he thought of young Jesus, talking to the priests beside the gleaming temple in Jerusalem. Yes, there had always been someone willing to live what they believed, who obeyed the voice of God, even when no one else did.

Grandmother's voice filtered into his thoughts. ''Like I said, it takes a very special kind of person to be a true child of God.''

Tony nodded slowly. Then he smiled. Grandmother was so wise. She probably knew everything there was to know about life. At least about those things that really mattered.

"How come you're so smart, Grandma?" he sighed.

The woman raised her eyebrows and glanced down at her grandson. "Me? Smart?" She laughed softly. "Let's just say I know the kinds of questions growing boys ask. After all, your father was your age once."

Tony looked startled. "He was? Oh, yeah! I guess he was. Funny. I always figured he was Dad from the very beginning."

Grandmother got up from her rocker and headed for the kitchen. "Dads are just little boys grown up. And if you're lucky, as you are, they never forget what it was like to be little."

The boy leaned his head against the beanbag and gazed into the fire. Would he remember what it was like to be little after he was all grown up? His mind wandered back to the scene beside the temple. He saw the young boy talking earnestly to the priests. An uncomfortable thought shadowed his reverie. Would the boy Jesus remember what it had been like to be God?

* * *

Dr. McFerren tapped the eraser end of his pencil against the smooth glass covering his broad oak desk. Kim sat across the room in his customary chair, watching the man intently.

The doctor spoke with some hesitancy. "I owe you an apology, Kim," he said, searching for words. "The last time you were here, I was not as kind to you as I should have been. I sit here demanding answers from you, yet I refused to answer your question."

Kim watched the man rise from his tall, overstuffed

76

chair and walk to a nearby window. "You asked me if I believed in God. Well, I do. In a way. You see, God and I, we sort of had a falling out, so to speak. If you're still interested, I'll tell you about it."

Kim nervously cleared his throat. "Dr. McFerren, I didn't mean to embarrass you. I just—"

"It's OK," the doctor interrupted. "You have every right to ask me any question you want. Don't feel bad about it. I should have been more professional and not acted as I did. Will you forgive me?"

Kim nodded, unsure of what to say. He was seeing a side of Dr. McFerren he'd never seen before. Here was the famous psychiatrist apologizing to a 13-year-old war orphan. Maybe the doctor wasn't such a bad guy after all.

Kim felt himself relax. "I forgive you Dr. McFerren," he said simply. "Thanks for asking."

The doctor smiled and turned back to the window. He closed his eyes for a long moment, then spoke slowly, thoughtfully.

"When I was a little boy, I lived with my mama and daddy down a dirty street in a dirty town surrounded by dirty factories. Every day I'd see my daddy get up before the sun, eat a bite of breakfast (if we were lucky enough that day to have something in the cupboards to eat), kiss my mama goodbye, and head out looking for work.

"When he'd reach the sidewalk in front of our apartment building, he'd turn and wave up at me. 'Take care of your mama, Billy,' he'd call out in the cold morning air. 'I be back before dark. You be a good boy, you hear?'

"I'd wave back to him and call, 'Don't you worry, Daddy. I take care of everything.'

"We attended church each week. The building was nothing to look at—paint peeling off the walls, hard flat-backed benches to sit on, a piano with a whole bunch of strings missing—but we worshiped God as best we could under the circumstances.

"I'd listen to the sermons, sing the songs, say my Bible verses, and try to ignore the rumbles in my tummy.

" 'God loves you,' the preacher would shout, 'and He's a-watchin' out for you.' I'd think, *If He loves me so much, why doesn't He bring me some food to eat?*

"My mama would always ask the blessing over what meals we had. I can hear her to this day. 'O, Lord, for this bounty we are thankful. And if it pleases Thee, may we have some bounty tomorrow, too. Ay—*MEN.*' "

The doctor stood silent for a minute, letting visions of the past drift slowly through his mind.

"One day, my daddy said to me, 'Billy, I have to go away for a little while. I got a job in a town south of here. But don't you worry. I'll be back before you even knows I'm gone.'

"He left early in the morning. I stood and waved at him. 'You take care of mama,' he called.

'Don't you worry, Daddy,' I called back, 'I'll take care of everything.' "

The doctor's hand pressed against the thick glass of the window. He continued speaking, his words becoming more and more strained.

"We got checks in the mail. Mama bought food. I got a brand new pair of shoes, even a bicycle. Not a new one, mind you, but like new. I thought to myself, God is lovin' us real good.

"Then the checks stopped coming, and after a few weeks this letter arrived in our mailbox saying how there'd been an accident and my daddy . . ."

Dr. McFerren's shoulders sagged under the awful

weight of memory. He turned and faced Kim. "They found a bus ticket in his pocket. He was going to come home that very day. Kim, my daddy was coming home to me."

The doctor's voice faltered. His eyes filled with unspeakable sorrow, then with a cold emotionless pain. Slowly he walked back to his chair and sat down. "So you see," he said looking across the room at his patient, "as far as that young, black, ghetto boy with the new shoes was concerned, God had died, too. It seems we have a lot in common, you and me, doesn't it?"

Kim sat motionless, staring at the doctor. He felt a familiar anger rising in his chest. What God could allow such sorrow? What eternal Being could create such a terrible world?

But then he remembered another little boy running along a dusty street. This child was God on earth—God's very own son. He would feel pain, fear, sorrow, just like everyone else.

Kim remembered seeing a deep longing in the eyes of the boy in Jerusalem, a longing like the one he'd felt since the war. Only someone who has known the pain of losing can truly understand another person's sorrow. Hadn't Tony said the boy would someday be sacrificed by the very people he came to love? He would know what it was like to lose. He would experience a lifetime of sorrow and pain.

Realization swept over the boy. His eyes filled with wonder and amazement. "That's why he came," he whispered. "That's why Jesus came!"

"What'd you say Kim?" Dr. McFerren glanced up from his desk. "Were you talking to me?"

The boy jumped to his feet. "Dr. McFerren, I think you need to know something, but I don't know how to tell you just yet. I'd like to think about it for a while, then I'll let you know what I find out, OK?''

The doctor was taken back by his patient's sudden outburst. "Well, sure, Kim, whatever you want to do."

The boy moved quickly toward the door. He stopped and turned to face the doctor. "We may be wrong, Dr. McFerren. I'll let you know."

The doctor studied the boy's face. "I'll look forward to hearing what you have to say, Kim."

After his patient had left, Dr. McFerren rose and walked slowly back to the window. Memories flowed once again through his tired mind. In the distance he could see his father standing on the sidewalk in front of the old apartment building. Lifting his hand to the glass, the doctor spoke in the stillness. "Don't worry, Daddy, I'll take care of everything."

The people on the street below paid no attention to the face in the window. Everyone was too busy with sorrows of his own.

Love Letter

THE school bell rang, sending its clanging call echoing up and down the long hallway as students hurried toward their assigned classrooms.

Tony sat down heavily at his desk and began fishing through his backpack, searching for the term paper he'd finished the night before. He smiled to himself as he read the title printed neatly across the top. "Molecular Fission: Is It All It's Cracked Up To Be?"

This ought to make his teachers happy. Not that they hadn't been satisfied with what he'd written before. His last report, "Black Holes: A Space Traveler's Gyude," had brought rave reviews, at least he thought that's what they were.

His English teacher had scrawled across the top of his paper, "I haven't the faintest idea what you're talking about, but your sentence structure is terrific."

Another had written, "Good work . . . I think!"

Even the school principal had gotten into the act. At the bottom of Tony's paper, "Solar Flares: The Untold Story," he'd written, "Does this student attend *our* facility?"

Tony didn't write to impress, although he liked it when people enjoyed reading the results of his long, hard studies.

He wrote in order to express himself. Inside his busy mind, facts and figures wandered about in crowded masses. Writing served to put facts in order, clarify ideas, and bring about decisions. Tony liked to watch his thoughts appear in neatly worded rows on his computer screen. Writing was his way of communicating to the world the things he couldn't say out loud.

A small white object landed on top of Tony's desk and slid into his lap. The boy wasn't sure where it had come from; classmates were swarming by his desk on their way to their seats. Maybe it was something important. Maybe someone dropped it by mistake.

He was about to get up and take the mystery object to his teacher when a word written on the tightly folded piece of paper caught his eye. His mouth dropped open. There, written in small, perfectly formed letters, was his name, *Tony*.

He looked around the room. No eyes met his. No one seemed to be aware that he had received the note.

He wasn't quite sure what to do. No one had ever written him a note in school before. Well, once Tie Li had sent him a letter. It was an assignment from her English teacher and had come with a pretend stamp and everything. Tie Li had placed it on his desk during recess.

But this was not his sister's handwriting. The boy squirmed in his seat. Someone in this very classroom had written him a real note, the kind he'd seen others pass around during boring lectures.

Tony stared at the object in his hand. Who would write him a note? Who would—

"Tony?" The teacher's voice jolted him to attention.

"I don't know . . ." Tony stammered.

"I beg your pardon?" The teacher looked up from her attendance record. "You don't know if you're here?"

Tony felt his face redden. Classmates began to snicker. "Come on, Tony," the teacher urged. "I need to know if you're here. If you're not here, then what are you doing in Tony Parks' desk, whoever you are?"

Waves of laughter washed over the classroom. Tony slid down in his chair until his knees jammed up against the underside of his desk. This was the most embarrassing moment of his life.

"Here," he said meekly.

"You're sure?" the teacher encouraged.

"Yes," Tony nodded, "I'm sure I'm here."

It took some time before order was restored again in the classroom. Tony held the note tightly in his fist, wondering how something so little could cause such a big problem. Whatever was written inside its tight folds had better be good. He'd paid a high price for it.

Tony kept the note safely tucked away in his backpack all afternoon. It wasn't until he was safely on the school bus, bumping and grinding along the country roads outside of town, that he dared look at it again.

"What that?" Tie Li asked, swaying with the movement of the bus and pointing toward the small wad of paper in her brother's hand.

Tony looked up and down the aisle, checking to make sure Kim was occupied with the passing scenery, then scrunched down in his seat. Tie Li scrunched down too.

"I got it today. Someone dropped it on my desk."

"Oh!" Tie Li's eyes filled with wonder. "A love letter! You lucky. I never got one."

Tony looked over at his little sister. "What makes you think it's a *love* letter?"

Tie Li lifted the folded paper and examined it closely. "See how it's bent this way, then that way? Only love letters look like that."

Tony grabbed the note and quickly brought it down to his lap again. "I don't love anybody at school."

"Well, someone love you." Tie Li nodded in agreement with herself. "Look like that person love you a *lot!* The more bending, the more love. Everybody know that."

Tony studied the object in his hand.

"Well, aren't you going to open it?" Kim's voice sounded over the roar of the bus.

Tony glanced up to see his brother's smiling face bending close to his. "Who knows? Maybe the future Mrs. Tony Parks signed it."

Tie Li giggled as Tony's face reddened again.

"Will you guys mind your own business? I'll read it when I'm good and ready!"

Kim leaned away in mock apology. "So sorry, Mr. Parks," he grinned, "but you'd better hurry. You're not getting any younger, you know."

Tony jammed the note deep into his backpack and stared at the seat back in front of him. He tried to ignore Tie Li, who sat blowing kisses in his direction. Her innocent fun finally got the best of his sense of humor. Wrestling her arms to her side, he held her firmly, trying not to laugh the rest of the way home.

That night after supper Tony went to the barn, where his dad was busy cleaning the cow pen. The boy grabbed a shovel. They worked in silence for a few minutes.

"Your studies all done?" Mr. Parks asked, stopping to rest against the tall wooden handle of his pitchfork.

Tony threw a load of manure into the large wheelbarrow standing in the corner of the pen. "Almost." The boy sat down on a feeding trough. "Dad, can I ask you something?"

Mr. Parks sat down beside his son. "What's on your mind, Tony? I noticed you were a little quiet at supper."

The boy shuffled his feet in the fresh straw lining the stall. "Dad, what would you do if you received a—a love letter?"

The man studied his son's face for a moment, then spoke quietly. "I guess I'd be happy someone cared for me enough to write down her feelings."

"You would?" Tony looked up in surprise. "You wouldn't be embarrassed or anything?"

"Well, maybe a little," the man said thoughtfully. "But love letters are very special. They're an expression of the heart."

"But," Tony hesitated, "is it OK for kids to write them to each other? I mean, isn't love just for people who get married and stuff like that?"

Mr. Parks smiled. "There are many different kinds of love, Tony. Sure, there's adult love that makes people want to get married and raise a family. That's the type of love your mother and I share.

"Then there's another kind of love that kids have for their parents, like you have for mother and me, and like I feel for Grandma.

"But when you're young, there's a kind of love that makes the world a beautiful place to be. As long as someone doesn't confuse this love with another kind, it can be very special."

Tony nodded. "You mean the way I love my computer?"

"Not exactly." Mr. Parks scratched his head and thought for a moment. He looked down at his son. Then with a twinkle in his eye he spoke. "Let's pretend there's a girl at your school who admired a certain boy at your school."

Tony stopped shuffling his feet and listened intently.

"She thinks he's very smart and kind and helpful. As a matter of fact, let's say she thinks he's the smartest, kindest, and most helpful boy in the entire class.

"One day she decides to tell him so. She doesn't want to embarrass him or herself by just standing up and saying, 'Hey, kid, I think you're smart, kind, and helpful, so I love you.' " Tony laughed out loud at the thought.

Mr. Parks continued. "Instead, she decides to write him a note and tell him what she thinks. That's a love letter."

"I see." Tony hesitated. "She writes him a note so he'll know how she feels?"

"That's right."

"And he should feel happy that she did that?"

"I would."

A broad smile spread across the young boy's face. Mr. Parks got up to resume his work. "There have been lots of love letters written in this world. Some are very mushy, filled with kisses and hugs and promises of undying affection. Some are more serious." The man threw a load of straw on the floor. "Even God wrote a love letter."

Tony's eyes opened wide. "God?"

"Sure. The Bible. It's a love letter too. It's filled with promises and words of affection, as well as stories of kings and prophets. It's the oldest love letter in all of history."

Tony sat for a moment, thinking of what his dad had said. If God had written a love letter, they can't be all bad. And now someone at school had cared enough to write him one this very day. That was neat!

The boy waved to his father as he headed out of the barn. "Thanks, Dad," he called over his shoulder. "I think I'll get back to my studies now."

The man watched his son disappear into the night. A smile creased his face. His little boy was growing up so fast.

Tony took the stairs to his room two at a time. Closing the door behind him, he jumped onto his bed and dug out the note from a dark corner of his backpack.

Slowly he unfolded it, being careful not to tear the soft paper. When it was open all the way, he discovered neatly formed words written in gently curving lines across the white creases. *I think you are a very nice boy. May I eat dinner with you tomorrow? Meet me at the fruit cooler at 12 o'clock. See you (I hope)! L.B.*

"L.B." Tony spoke quietly. "Who is L.B.?"

Rendezvous

TIE LI looked up at Kim, then at Tony. She searched their somber faces for some sign of life.

"What wrong with you guys?" she implored, shouting to be heard above the whining roar of the school bus engine. "This morning you both very quiet. You sick?"

The boys continued to stare in two different directions, lost in thought.

"I think there is a lion on the school bus. See? Over there? Yes, there's big lion going to school with us!"

No response.

Tie Li shifted her position annoyingly. She always looked forward to each morning's bus ride to school because it offered her a chance to sit between her two favorite people and tell them all the exciting things going on in her life. But today she may as well have been sitting between two lumps of clay.

"I getting married today," she said. "You want to come?"

Nothing.

The girl decided to try a new approach. Grabbing her

throat, she opened her mouth, stuck out her tongue, and began making gurgling noises as she swayed back and forth. Then with a final dramatic groan, she collapsed across Kim's lap, her schoolbooks tumbling onto the floor.

Kim looked down at the still form sprawled over his legs. He shook his head slowly from side to side. Glancing at Tony, he spoke somberly. "Too many chocolate chip cookies. They'll get you every time."

Tony nodded in agreement. "And she was so young. We'd better tell the bus driver to stop so we can bury this poor little girl out there in a snowbank."

The two sat in silence for a moment, then both smiled and shouted, "Dibs on her lunch!"

Tie Li sat up and started hammering her brothers with playful fists. "You don't care that I die! You just want to eat my food. Well, never mind. I alive again!"

The boys laughed at their sister's reprimand and helped gather her scattered books and papers. But even in the merriment of the moment, both had serious thoughts crowding their minds. Foremost in Tony's plans was his upcoming rendezvous with the mysterious L.B. And Kim had decided that today he would find the body behind the face—that sneering, hateful face—that had greeted him his first day at school.

A living tide of children surged down the hallway as the first bell rang. Kim stood at the door of his classroom, searching the faces passing by. He'd done this before. Each day each class would find him here, looking for a hint of hate hiding in the eyes of those entering the room.

But it seemed the face had simply disappeared. No eyes met his with the type of intense emotion he'd seen that first day. No voice sounded as bitter. No lips so thinly drawn.

Could hate change a person so much that he'd be unrecognizable without it?

"He's not here." A man's voice spoke from behind Kim. Turning, the boy saw Mr. Carlton, his teacher, leaning against a bookcase.

Kim studied the man's face. "You know who he is? You know who tripped me? Why didn't you—?"

"Come to my office, Kim. I'd like to talk to you for a minute." The man led Kim down the long hallway to an empty room beside the main entrance of the school building. Closing the door, he motioned for Kim to have a seat. Mr. Carlton took his place behind an old metal desk, its surface piled high with students' papers, teaching forms, class schedules, and a ceramic mug with a big yellow smiley face printed on it. To one side rested a potted plant adorned with brown, wilted leaves.

"I need to water this silly thing a little more often, wouldn't you say?" the man mused, fingering the dry, parched foliage.

"Yes, sir," Kim responded quietly.

The man sat back in his chair, his eyes slowly scanning the cluttered inventory of his desk. "So many things to do, and no time to do them." Mr. Carlton sighed. "Sometimes I wonder what I'm supposed to work on more, cluttered desks or cluttered minds."

Kim watched his teacher rub his chin thoughtfully. He sensed the man had something to say, but it was hard for him to start.

"Mr. Carlton, you brought me here for a reason. Have I done something wrong?"

The man smiled. "No, you haven't done anything except maybe being born at the wrong time in the wrong place."

"What do you mean by that?"

"Kim, because of who you are and what you represent, you have enemies. I know it's sad, but it's true."

"Are you talking about the boy who tripped me?"

Mr. Carlton nodded. "He's got this wild notion that nations fight nations in wars for good and noble purposes that people of one race have the God-given responsibility to fight people of other races until everyone thinks and acts the same way. So he keeps right on fighting, even after a war ends, because in his mind it really hasn't ended."

Kim's forehead creased in frustration. "Where did he learn such crazy thinking?"

"From his father. You see, his dad had a brother who was killed in a war. All this happened before the boy was born. But his dad had such hate in his heart for the people responsible for his brother's death that he carried his bitterness into his married life and into the heart and mind of his young son. After what happened the other day, the boy was suspended from school."

Kim shook his head. "I know what it's like to feel hate, but I didn't know you could teach someone else to share your feelings. After the war came to my country I wanted to destroy those responsible for what was happening. But my dad kept telling me, 'Don't hate, son. You only end up hurting the people that need your love.' "

"Your father was a very wise man, Kim," Mr. Carlton said soberly. "Every boy should have a father like that."

Kim was silent for a moment. "I'd like to talk to the boy who tripped me. Will you tell me where he is?"

The man stood to his feet. "I'll do better than that. I'll take you to him. I've scheduled a film to be shown in class. We've got an hour. It should give us just enough time."

Kim grabbed his coat from his locker and followed his

teacher to the parking lot. They got into Mr. Carlton's car and drove north, away from the school. Kim watched snow-covered streets speed by beyond the frosted window of Mr. Carlton's station wagon. He felt excitement gnawing at the pit of his stomach. Finally he was going to have his chance. He was going to meet the boy behind the face.

The car stopped in front of a small, brick house half hidden behind a row of wide evergreen trees. Mr. Carlton switched off the engine and sat back in his seat with a heavy sigh. "His name is Ted. His parents call him Teddy."

Kim studied the long walkway leading to the house. He reached up to open the car door, then hesitated. "Aren't you coming, Mr. Carlton?"

The man remained motionless, staring out the window. "You go ahead. I'll join you in a minute."

Kim opened the door and slid off the seat. Snow crunched under his boots as he made his way toward the house. Dark, faded curtains hung limply in each window. Cold gusts of wind sent miniature snowy tornadoes wandering aimlessly across the front yard. Somewhere, far away, a dog barked at an imagined intruder. Kim shivered under his coat and scarf.

At the door, the boy looked back toward the car. Mr. Carlton sat watching him. The teacher.

Kim's gloved hand knocked against the storm door. A noisy rattle echoed in the entryway.

"Who is it?" A woman's voice called out from somewhere in the house.

"It's Kim Parks."

"Kim who?"

The boy cleared his throat. "I'm Kim Parks, from Ted's school."

Kim jumped as the door cracked open against its chain

lock. A frowning face appeared looking down at him. "You go to school with Teddy?"

"Yes, ma'am. I'm in his class."

The door closed, then opened again, a little wider this time. "What do you want?"

"I'd like to see Ted, if you don't mind. I'd like to talk to him for a minute."

Kim watched as the woman studied him carefully. When she seemed satisfied that he was not a threat to her or the house, she opened the door the rest of the way. "He's not here right now, but I'm expecting him back any moment. You can wait inside if you'd like. Just have a seat over there."

Kim walked to a chair by the window and sat down. "Thank you," he said, looking around the room. "You have a nice house."

The woman closed the door. "It'll do. So, you say you're a friend of my Teddy's?"

Kim frowned. "I guess that's up to him. We sort of got off to a bad start. We have some unfinished business to attend to."

The back door of the house slammed shut as footsteps echoed down the short hallway leading to the kitchen. "Mom, I'm back. I hope I got the right kind of soap. I think every company in the world makes soap."

The woman smiled. "I'm sure you did. Hey, son, you've got company. Says he goes to school with you."

"Oh, yeah?" The boy's voice grew louder as he moved through the kitchen, toward the living room. "I don't know anybody who'd come to visit me now."

Kim stood as the voice drew closer.

"Maybe he brought an assignment or—"

The boy rounded the corner, then stopped when he saw

93

Kim. "You!" he said, his lips forming a tight line across his teeth. His eyes narrowed into a cold, harsh stare. Fists formed at his sides. "What are *you* doing here?"

Battlefield

THE transformation shocked Kim. At first the boy had appeared normal, like any other kid. But now the face was twisted, strained, reflecting a deep, hurting rage.

Kim raised his hands, palms up. "I just want to talk to you, Ted, that's all."

The boy moved toward his unexpected guest. "You want to talk? I'll talk to you. With these!" Fists swung past Kim's face. He jumped back, stumbling over the chair.

"Teddy!" the woman screamed. "Teddy, what are you doing?"

Kim continued to move away, trying to keep out of range of the boy's fists. "Why do you hate me so much? I didn't kill your uncle. I wasn't even born yet! Neither were you. How can you hate me for something I didn't do?"

"Teddy!" Mr. Carlton's voice rang out from the doorway. "Stop this right now!"

The boy glanced at the man, somewhat taken aback. "What do you mean, stop? I got him. I can make him pay for Uncle Bobby's death. They killed him! Now they'll pay!''

Ted lunged toward Kim. His fist brushed the boy's chin and smashed into the lamp beside the coffee table. The woman cried out as glass shattered across the floor.

Without hesitating, Ted dove once more toward Kim, a raspy cry escaping from behind clenched teeth. ''Murderer!'' he screeched. ''Monster! You'll pay. It's all your fault!''

Strong arms grabbed Ted and wrestled him to the floor. ''No!'' Mr. Carlton shouted. ''Leave him alone. I was wrong, Teddy. I was wrong.''

Kim's mouth dropped open as he watched his teacher pin the screaming boy against the living room rug.

''Teddy,'' the man shouted, ''Uncle Bob was killed by a bullet from one man's gun, fighting for a cause that ended long ago.''

Ted struggled to escape Mr. Carlton's grasp. ''But you said those people killed him. You said they were pigs, monsters, that none of them should be allowed to live.''

Tears filled the man's eyes as he lifted the boy and held him tightly. ''They didn't kill Uncle Bob. The war did. Human violence pulled the trigger. We all fought a common enemy. We are all equally guilty for what happened.''

Ted stopped his wild struggling and looked up into the face of the man holding him. ''What are you saying? Did Uncle Bobby die for no reason at all? Was his life just wasted? Didn't you love him? Didn't you love your own brother?''

Mr. Carlton's shoulders sagged as sobs wrung the energy from his arms. He sat down heavily on the floor, his hands slipping from around the boy's waist. ''I loved him so much." His voice was thin, broken. "He was my hero. I worshiped him."

Mrs. Carlton sat down beside her husband. She gently placed her arms around his shoulders.

The man looked at Kim. "When my brother died, I was destroyed inside. I couldn't go on living without him. The only thing that kept me sane was a vow to revenge his death.

"As the years passed, I thought I'd outgrown my hate. But I see that I simply passed it on to Teddy." The man gazed into the eyes of his son. "I didn't mean to hurt you. I didn't mean to fill you with such hate. Teddy, Kim's a victim of that war just as we are. Just as Uncle Bobby was. The fighting continues, only now with different soldiers, different bombs, different blood. Kim lost his mom and dad in fires set by anger and greed. There's no victory in war. Only loss. Only pain."

Kim glanced at Ted's face. He saw the hate, the anger, the pain slowly ease, leaving eyes filled with questions. "Dad?" the boy whispered, pressing close to his father, "teach me how to stop hating. Teach me to love again."

Mr. Carlton wrapped his son in his arms. He looked over at Kim, his eyes pleading for forgiveness. The boy smiled and nodded. In this home, on this battlefield, the war was finally over.

* * *

Tony glanced up at the clock. He felt sure those long, thin hands had decided to remain in the ten-till-twelve position. Glancing back at his geography book, he read the sentence at the top of the page for the eighth time. The boy thought of the note hiding deep in his pocket. What was he going to say when he met this mysterious L.B. person?

He remembered what his dad had said earlier—that he

was supposed to feel honored when someone cared enough to write down her or his feelings. Even God wrote love letters! Tony thought of the Creator walking with Adam and Eve beside the lake in the Garden of Eden. Yes, God certainly had the ability to write love letters. Every word He said that day sounded like one.

A sobering thought dampened his daydreaming. What if he didn't like this L.B.? What if she didn't even exist? What if the note was a fake, written by a bunch of guys trying to make him look like a fool? What if?

The noon bell sang its piercing song, accompanied by desks slamming shut, children cheering, and hurrying feet heading for the door. It was time to find the answers. L.B., whoever she was, would be waiting. The mystery was about to be solved.

"Tony, may I speak to you for a moment?" The teacher's voice called out as he reached the door.

"Uh . . . well . . . could it wait until after lunch? I'm . . . uh . . . really hungry." Tony stumbled over his words, not wanting to sound disrespectful, yet fearing he'd miss his all-important appointment at the fruit cooler.

"It won't take but a few minutes," Mrs. Lawson smiled. "I had a question on your last term paper. You remember, the one you wrote about South America? 'Chili: More Than Just Stew.' "

"Oh, yeah." Tony eyed the clock. "Did I leave something out?"

"No, not really, although you mentioned things about the country I've never heard of."

"Like what?" Tony stood on one foot, then the other, trying not to look impatient.

"Like the paragraph outlining the government's plan to equip remote military bases with high-speed computers that''—she picked up Tony's report—''and I quote, 'will aid in the security of shoreline defense installations, allowing for a reduction in personnel needed to monitor movement of trade goods between ports of call and inland business centers,' end quote. Tony, where did you get this kind of information?''

The boy cleared his throat. ''On my computer. I just logged on to the main data processing center at the American Embassy down there and read the reports. The government's donating their old outdated computers to their education program. Isn't that neat?''

''But isn't it illegal to tap into government data files?''

Tony looked shocked at the accusation. ''The minister of information said I could get whatever I wanted from their data base if I figured out their password. He didn't think I could. But I did, on my first log-on attempt. The rest was easy.''

Mrs. Lawson looked at the report, then at Tony. ''And what was the password?''

The boy smiled and moved toward the door. ''Stew,'' he called over his shoulder. ''You know, the kind you eat?''

The teacher watched her student disappear from view. She shook her head slowly back and forth. ''Stew,'' she repeated absently.

Tony raced down the hallway toward the crowded lunchroom. He could hear laughter and loud talking as hungry mouths munched on assorted nourishments packed earlier that day by loving moms or dads. Would L.B. still be there? Maybe she got mad because he was late. He hurried his steps.

Tony made his way to the fruit cooler by the wall at the far end of the bright, sunny eating area. He stopped at one end of the long cooler and pretended to inspect the fruit lying in orderly rows under the frosty sliding glass doors.

No one seemed to pay him any attention. The boy began to feel disappointment rising in his chest. He was too late. L.B. had already given up on him. He slid the cooler door open and selected a big, ripe apple. He held the fruit in his hand, inspecting it for bruises.

Someone spoke. "I like apples too. My favorites are the big yellow ones."

Tony glanced up. The girl looked familiar; seemed as if he'd seen her someplace before, but he wasn't sure. "Yeah, they're good," he shrugged, trying to brush her off. "You want one?"

The girl smiled. "Yes, please."

Tony grabbed a yellow apple from the pile and handed it to her. "Enjoy," he mumbled, searching the sea of faces for someone looking his direction.

"Do you remember me?" the girl persisted. "We sat together on the school bus a week or so ago. You were reading something about dinosaurs."

Tony nodded weakly. "Oh, yeah, I remember." The boy walked along the cooler, watching for signs of the mystery writer.

The girl followed close behind. "I bet you don't even remember my name," she teased.

"Sure I do," Tony frowned, wishing the girl would go away. "It was . . . was . . . Laura something-or-other."

"Hey, you do remember!" The girl's smile broadened. "At least part of it. I'm Laura Bates." She repeated her name, slower this time. "Laura Bates."

Tony shrugged. "Oh, yeah, Laura Ba—" The boy stopped in his tracks. His lips moved, forming the name he'd just heard. He turned to face the girl with the yellow apple. "You're L.B.?"

Laura spread her arms and bowed slightly. "In the flesh."

Tony closed his eyes and leaned back against the cooler. "I'm such a jerk," he sighed.

"Well, you're a late jerk," Laura Bates snickered playfully.

"I'm sorry," Tony groaned. "Mrs. Lawson wanted to talk to me."

"No harm done," the girl said. "I hope you're not disappointed that I'm who I am. You probably had imagined that some beautiful, intelligent, real knockout of a girl wrote that note. But it was just me."

"I didn't know what to think," Tony admitted. "No one ever wrote me a note before."

"Really?" Laura seemed surprised.

"Well, sometimes my mom puts little messages in my lunch, but they don't count. She's just my mom."

Laura shrugged. "Moms are good. At least most moms are, I guess."

Tony saw a frown shadow the girl's face. Before he could say anything, Laura motioned to him. "Hey, there's an empty table over there. You ready to eat?"

Tony nodded and followed the girl across the room to a table by the window. A few classmates whistled as they passed, but Tony didn't pay any attention. Maybe it was his nature to notice when things weren't quite right. Maybe it was all the time he'd spent with Tie Li that had made him more aware of other people's feelings. Whatever the reason, he knew Laura Bates was carrying some kind of sadness in her heart.

He watched the girl unwrap her sandwich and lay it on her napkin. The bread was dry, crumbly. It looked as though it had been thrown together at the last minute.

"Thank you for eating with me," she said softly. "I was right. You are a real gentleman."

Tony smiled. The mystery had been solved. But another, much more puzzling secret lay waiting on Laura Bates' napkin.

Fishers of Men

I'M ALMOST ready.'' Tony's fingers tapped rhythmically on the keyboard. "Just a minute or two."

Tie Li and Kim sat by the workbench watching their brother enter data in his computer. It was Sunday. The chores were done, homework had been attacked and completed early, and Mom and Dad Parks were visiting Grandma at the cabin. *Voyager* stood ready in one corner of the workshop, its electronic innards humming contentedly, lights glowing as its inventor keyed in coordinates for its next journey back in time.

"So, Tony," Kim said, his chin resting on his hands, "how did your date with the mysterious L.B. go? Was she as beautiful as you hoped she'd be?"

Tony continued typing. "She was real nice. I like her."

Tie Li's eyes opened wide. "Ohhhhh," she breathed. "I think my brother has girlfriend!"

The boy smiled. "Well, she's a girl, and she's my friend, but let's not get carried away."

Kim laughed. "*We* won't get carried away if you don't."

Tony's face reddened just a little. "Come on, you guys. Can't a fellow have a friend?"

"My dad used to tell me about a friend he had when he was a boy like us," Kim encouraged. "That worked out all right."

"There, you see?" Tony nodded. "What'd I tell you?"

"Yeah, and you know what happened?"

"What?"

"They got married."

Tony sighed and looked over at his brother. "Thanks for your support."

"Laura Parks," Tie Li said thoughtfully. "Has a nice chime to it."

"Will you guys stop with the matchmaking already?" Tony begged. "You're getting me all nervous."

Kim and Tie Li exchanged winks. "OK," Tie Lie agreed, then added, "we don't want to embarrass you and the little missus."

Tony sighed. Trying to be friends with someone sometimes carried a high price. But he did like Laura. She was sweet and kind, and besides, she thought he was wonderful. Tony liked that combination in a person.

"There," the boy said, studying the screen. "That should do it. Let's get out of here before you have me married off or something."

The three took their positions in *Voyager*. Moments later they were speeding back through the years heading for a place called Galilee.

"Well, at least I don't think it's going to rain," Kim said, stepping down from the machine and eyeing the clear blue canopy of sky stretching across a wide expanse of shimmering water. "I'm glad your aim is good." He pointed toward the nearby shoreline. "A couple dozen more feet and we'd have been riding in *Voyager* the boat.''

Tony snickered. ''I may not be able to control the weather, but I can tell this machine where to land. It hasn't failed me yet.''

Tie Li looked out over the water. ''Where are we, Tony? Is this ocean?''

The boy activated the machine's solar recharge switch. ''No. We're on the north shore of the Sea of Galilee. It's sort of like a great big lake.'' He pointed south. ''Down there is where the Jordan River begins. Remember? We saw the Jordan with Simon. It was when that man's donkey talked to him.''

''Oh, yes,'' Tie Li giggled. ''We told Simon to tell us what the donkey said. He was very silly.''

''A donkey talked?'' Kim questioned.

''It's a long story,'' Tony nodded. ''Tie Li will tell you about it sometime. It was pretty funny. Well, Simon didn't think it was all that hilarious, but we did.''

The three walked along the beach for a few minutes enjoying the clean, fresh air and the beauty of the green, rolling hills. They watched fishing boats move slowly among the gentle swells, their nets hanging limp in the sunshine, drying.

''Most fishing here is done early in the morning, or at night.'' Tony pointed at the bobbing boats. ''They've probably been working for hours. I think they're just about finished for the day.''

''What are we going to see here?'' Kim queried, surveying the peaceful mountains surrounding the blue waters of Galilee.

Tony sat down on the old, weatherworn hull of an abandoned boat. ''The boy we saw in Jerusalem has grown up. He's 30 years old now. The Book said he came here to find some men to help him teach people how to love each other and not fight all the time. He wants to tell them about God, his Father.''

''Here?'' Kim looked around. ''I don't see anybody I'd trust with that kind of responsibility. Who can he find in a place like this?''

One of the boats riding the waves just beyond the breakers turned and floated away from the others. The men on board guided their little craft along the shore and finally beached it beside some other boats resting on the rocky sand. Nearby, rugged, sun-browned men bent low in the morning light, mending tears in the intricate folds of their nets.

''I think the fish knew we were coming,'' a big, rough-looking man on the boat called to his friends. ''It seems fish are smarter than we are!'' The men laughed and nodded. One called out, ''So the great Simon Peter came up emptyhanded again, eh? Maybe the little fishes didn't like your ugly face. You scared them away.''

''No,'' the man on the boat grinned, ''they were stunned by my beauty. After seeing me, they all fell in love and sank to the bottom.'' He pointed toward his taunters. ''Tomorrow I'll send you guys out. They'll come up to see what strange-looking men are trying to catch them. Our nets will be full!''

Laughter echoed along the shoreline. The fishermen secured their boat and joined the others by the nets.

''What a way to make a living,'' the big man sighed. ''I should be in Jerusalem knocking Roman heads. Herod can fish all night while I sit around ruling the world and collecting taxes.''

''Wonderful,'' another man spoke up, ''Peter the king. He'd probably have me serving his royal dinner.''

"Not a bad plan, my dear brother Andrew," Peter chuckled, thrusting his chin in the air and striking an aristocratic pose. "And what, pray tell, would you prepare for my dining pleasure?"

"Fish!" Andrew sneered, holding up an imaginary plate. "Boiled fish, fried fish, scalloped fish, fish milk, fish eggs, and for dessert"—he paused for effect—"fish tarts!"

Peter held his stomach and fell with a thud onto the sand. "No, no, no," he moaned. "Where are the melons? Where is the honey?" He grabbed hold of a pair of feet and looked up pleadingly. "And where are—?"

The man whose legs he was clutching was not one of his buddies. Simon's face reddened as the stranger started to laugh. "I don't have any melons or honey, but I've got some day-old bread. Want some?"

Peter stumbled to his feet. "I'm sorry, friend," he said, nervously brushing sand from his arms. "I thought you were my brother."

The stranger smiled. "That's a compliment. I'd like to be your brother."

A man by the nets called out good-naturedly, "Watch what you say, friend. If you want Simon Peter as a member of your family, you'd better be prepared to fight for what's yours."

Laughter erupted from the little assembly.

"I accept the challenge," the stranger smiled. "Besides, I need a brother like Simon Peter. He can teach me many things."

Peter looked at the man in surprise. "You *need* a brother like me? I don't understand."

The man nodded. "Yes, I need you." He pointed at Andrew. "And you too." He motioned toward those standing by the nets. "I need all of you."

The men looked at each other. "What do you need us for?"

"What do you do for a living?" the stranger asked.

"We fish," one answered. "Anyone can see that."

"And what do you catch?"

Simon was getting a little upset with whatever game this man was playing. "We catch fish," he said flatly. "Anything wrong with that?"

The man nodded. "Not a thing." He stopped and studied the big man's face. "If that's all you want to catch."

Peter held the stranger's gaze. How could this man know what he was feeling inside? Just last night, out on the water, he had wondered to himself if there was more to life than the endless cycle of sailing and fishing, selling, and sailing again. He longed for something meaningful to fill his days. He was not an educated man, but longed for a life of worth, of value. He longed to feel good about himself. In his deepest heart he hungered to be a part of something bigger than his little world beside the sea.

Simon Peter looked at his friends, then back at the man on the shore. "Sir, what would you have us catch?"

The stranger spoke softly, his voice carrying to the ears of every man standing nearby. "Follow me," he said, "and I will make you fishers of men."

Peter hesitated. "And when we catch these men, then what do we do?"

The man smiled. "Love them. Teach them. Save them."

"But we are only fishermen. How can we do such a thing?"

The stranger pointed toward the fishing boats. "In God's work it's not so much the fisherman as it is the net."

Peter studied the man's face for a long moment. "Sir," he said, "you seem to know what is in my heart. If your work is of God, I would like to help."

"Me too." Andrew joined in. "Besides, someone would have to watch out for my hotheaded brother here."

Two others walked from their nets and stood by the stranger. "We are James and John, the sons of Zebedee. We only know how to fish. But if you will teach us, we want to learn how to help our fellowman. Would you take us, too?"

The man on the shore nodded. "There's a place for each one of you in my work. If you are willing to leave your families, your homes, your nets for a while, and follow me, I will teach you, guide you."

"You know our names," Peter said quietly. "What do we call you?"

The stranger smiled. "I am Jesus of Nazareth. And from this day forward you will be called my disciples."

The four men and the stranger turned and walked away, leaving empty boats and torn nets behind. For these fishermen, the sea would never be the same again.

Things to Come

TONY, Tie Li, and Kim walked in silence along the snow-covered path leading to Grandmother's cabin. Each was lost in thought, playing the scene by Galilee over and over in their minds.

They felt something important had happened. Jesus of Nazareth had traded the warm security of his father's carpenter shop for the cold reality of life as the Son of God. Now he'd chosen simple fishermen to help him save a hurting world.

"I don't think it's going to work," Kim spoke, his words muffled by the scarf covering his chin and lips. "Who's going to believe them? I mean, they're just ordinary people like us. Nothing special."

Tony studied the smooth outline of Bentley's pond etched in the pasture beside the path. Each time he walked by here, a numbing fear gripped his heart. The boy glanced down at his little sister stumbling through the drifts, trying her best to keep up. Tony shivered, not so much from the cold as from the memory. "Those fishermen are going to be shocked when they find out who he really is. They think

110

Jesus is just a kind man, a teacher, someone who wants to help people. They don't know he's the Son of God."

Tie Li sat down heavily on a log. "Wait," she called to her brothers. "I'm too tired. We rest for a minute, OK?"

Tony and Kim stopped and looked back at the little girl sprawled across the log. Puffs of steam rose with each breath as Tie Li tried to force oxygen into her aching lungs.

"We're sorry, Tie Li," Kim grinned, a little embarrassed. "We forgot you don't have long legs like ours. We'll rest with you for a while."

The boys joined their sister on the log. Tony looked around uneasily. "This place gives me the creeps. I keep thinking about when Tie Li took her little dip through the ice earlier this winter."

The girl smiled up at her brother. "But you save me, Tony," she encouraged. "You ran very fast and got Mr. Bentley and the rope. You are a hero."

"Some hero," Tony sighed. "Who do you think got you out there in the first place?"

"You just wanted me to have a fun time."

Tony gazed out at the frozen surface for a long moment. He remembered another pond, this one surrounded by green grass and brightly colored flowers. Two beautiful beings had stopped to drink the cool, clear waters that splashed along the sparkling shore. Their world had broken up under their feet too. For generations, the people of earth had needed someone on the shore, ready with a rope, ready to save them.

"I think we all walk on thin ice from time to time." Tony kicked at a mound of snow beside his foot. "I think we all need a hero."

Kim nodded. "That's what the fishermen were looking

for. They must think Jesus of Nazareth can be their hero. I hope He can.''

The three sat in silence. A cold breeze whispered through the pine needles overhead.

Suddenly Tony jumped to his feet. He stood very still, gazing toward the forest on the other side of the pond. ''Hey, you guys, listen!''

Kim and Tie Li looked at each other, then at their brother.

Tony pointed in the direction of a clump of trees. ''There, did you hear that?''

''Hear what?'' Tie Li asked, leaning forward expectantly, trying to catch the sound her brother was talking about.

''There it is again!'' Tony called out, his voice rising with excitement.

Kim walked over and stood beside his brother. ''I don't hear anything.''

''Come on!'' Tony raced down the path. Kim and Tie Li hurried close behind. The children ran toward the woods, leaving clouds of swirling snow in their wake.

At the base of the evergreens, Tony stopped and lifted his hand for silence. Kim and Tie Li froze in their tracks, their vaporized breath drifting in the stillness.

From deep in the forest came a soft, warbling sound, its sweet melody filtering through the barren branches above.

''It's a robin!'' Tony's face radiated with the excitement that comes with finding an old, long-lost friend. ''Do you hear him?''

The children nodded. ''Is robin good?'' Tie Li ventured.

Tony almost shouted. ''Is he ever! This means *spring* is coming. This means the snow will melt soon, the air will warm up, all the little forest animals will run around again.

Winter's almost over! It'll soon be spring!''

Tie Li jumped up and down, her gloved hands slapping together. "Spring is coming, spring is coming!" she called out, her voice as happy as the robin's. "Soon my nose stop freezing off."

Kim watched his sister race into the woods, searching for the treetop songster. He felt her excitement, her enthusiasm for life. Standing at the edge of the forest, he began to realize something very important about himself, something he'd forgotten. Tie Li depended on him, Tony, and the others in her life for the joy she felt inside. Without love, her world would be dark, cold, frightening. But he could change all that. He could make her happy, contented. He was important to her. No, not just important; he was necessary.

Kim thought of the man from Nazareth. This carpenter wanted to bring love to a whole world. He wanted to change people's lives. Yes, Jesus wanted to be necessary too.

"Kim, come look!" Tie Li's happy voice carried in the cold air. "I found the robin. He's very beautiful. Hurry, come look!"

Kim smiled to himself as he walked into the forest. How happy he was to be able, after years of separation, to answer his sister's call.

* * *

"A robin? Really?" Grandmother Parks set her cup of steaming herb tea on its saucer and looked up in surprise. "I thought I heard one this morning, but I wasn't sure."

Tony nodded. "Yup, in the woods by Bentley's Pond. Tie Li saw it too."

The little girl pulled her gloves off with her teeth. "It pretty," she said with enthusiasm. "A robin sings a nice song."

"Did you see it too, Kim?" Grandmother asked.

"Almost," came the reply from in front of the fireplace. "Some little wild animal scared it away before I could get there."

Tie Li snickered. "I tried to climb tree for better look, but robin flew away."

Grandmother laughed. "Don't worry, Kim, you'll get another chance. We have lots of robins around here in the spring and summer."

Tony opened the refrigerator door and stood eyeing its contents. "Last year we had a nest in the birch beside the barn. Grandmother, don't you have any cookies?"

The woman pointed toward a large jar resting on the counter. "Over there," she said. "Help yourself."

Tony closed the refrigerator door and hurried to the other side of the kitchen. He reached into the jar and pulled out a big red apple.

"Enjoy," Grandmother grinned, a familiar twinkle in her eye.

Tony smiled and polished the fruit against his sweater. "The old apples in the cookie jar trick," he laughed. "You never change, Grandmother."

"Of course not," the woman replied, taking a sip of tea. "I love you too much to do that."

Tony positioned himself into the large beanbag beside the fire and sank his teeth into the juicy fruit. The sweet liquid tickled his tongue and filled his nostrils with the fresh scent of cider. "Delicious," he acknowledged. "Great cookie."

The crackling fire flickered happily as the afternoon wore on. Grandmother told stories from years gone by, adventure stories that moved on buckboards and paddle wheelers, stories about love and courage, about strong men

114

and faithful women, about a little girl who traveled west with her family, toward the mountains and the unknown.

Tony, Tie Li, and Kim sat spellbound at Grandmother's knee, drinking in every word. In their mind's eye, they could see the prairies stretching out to the horizon, feel the hot wind pressing against their straining muscles, hear the faltering steps of animals gone lame on the rugged trails.

"And that's how my mother, Tony's great-grandmother, arrived at her new home beside the river. New adventures loomed just around the corner. Life in Red Rose Valley would not be easy, but they'd come too far to ever go back again." Grandmother let out a long sigh. "I'll save those stories for another time. You children must get back to the farm before it gets dark."

Tony slowly stood to his feet, stretching muscles that hadn't moved for hours. "You tell the best stories in the world, Grandmother," he said. "You're better than television."

"Well, thank you," the woman smiled. "At least I don't have any commercials."

Tie Li pulled her coat down from the hook by the door. "I have story too," she hinted.

"You do?" Grandmother encouraged.

"Yes. It about a man who walked along a sea and asked some fishermen to help him make people happy."

The woman glanced at Tony, then back at Tie Li. "And then what happened?"

"I don't know," the little girl giggled. "But I'll tell you when I find out."

"OK," Grandmother agreed. "I'm looking forward to it."

Kim wrapped his scarf tightly around his neck. "Me

too,'' he said, tucking the loose ends under his collar. ''There's someone else who needs to know. It's important to both of us.''

The Accused

LAURA Bates sat on the edge of her bed thumbing through a library book. Every once in a while she'd glance out the window toward the long curving driveway leading from the main road, through the orchard, to the courtyard in front of her home.

In the far distance she could see cars moving along the interstate that paralleled the river east of town.

"Late again," she sighed, letting her gaze settle on the empty driveway. "Imagine that."

Closing the book, she pressed her feet into the warm, fuzzy slippers waiting at the foot of her bed and shuffled out into the hallway. The late afternoon sun reflected on the smooth wooden floor and illuminated the gold leaf-framed pictures hanging on the wall.

Laura moved slowly, gazing up at each image. At one portrait she paused. A sad smile nudged the corners of her mouth as her dark eyes scrutinized the handsome face looking down at her. In a voice not much above a whisper she said, "Hi, Papa."

She stood for a long time studying the face in the

picture. How long had it been now? Five, six years? It was hard to remember. She'd been so young.

"Laura? Are you home?" A woman's voice called from the landing below. "The traffic was just dreadful. You must be famished."

Laura walked to the top of the stairs and watched her mother move between the coatroom and the entrance to the dining area. "Here I am," the girl called.

Mrs. Bates stopped and smiled up at her daughter. "There's my lovely Laura. Did you have a good day?"

Before Laura could answer, the woman turned and disappeared into the kitchen. "You won't believe the trouble I had today." A disembodied voice echoed through the foyer. "I mean, it was just one thing after another. You'd think that silly company could do without me for a few hours, but no. They're all a bunch of babies."

Laura sat down on the top step, her chin resting in her hands. Mother never had a *good* day. Never. So why didn't she just stop working? She didn't need the money.

"You want french fries or soup for supper? Oh, never mind. We don't have any soup. Remind me to pick some up tomorrow."

Laura walked down the stairs and stood in the doorway leading to the kitchen. She watched as her mother tried to wrestle a frying pan from the wide drawer under the stove. The pan was caught on something. The more the woman pulled, the tighter it wedged itself in the tangle of cookware.

"Want me to help you?" Laura asked, moving toward the stove.

"No!" Mrs. Bates fought to control her rising anger. "No, I'll do it." She pulled hard on the handle. "I'm not

118

going to let some stupid frying pan keep me from making you supper.''

"It's OK, Mom." Laura sounded frightened. "Here, I can eat this cereal. I don't mind."

The woman gritted her teeth. "I said french fries and that's what you're going to get!''

Suddenly the pan shot out of the cupboard as the drawer's hinges gave way. Pots, bread tins, and mixing bowls scattered across the floor. Mrs. Bates fell backward against a table, sending spoons, knives, a box of recipes, dishes, and assorted cooking utensils, smashing against the cupboards on the far side of the kitchen.

The woman screamed in rage. Laura raced toward the table, her voice thin, shaking. "I'll clean it up, Mother. Don't worry about it. I'll clean it up!''

Mrs. Bates rose, her body tight, awkward. "Leave it. *Leave it!*''

"It's OK. Really. I'll clean it up."

Laura felt something hard slam into her face. "I said *leave* it!''

The impact of the blow forced the girl to her knees. Broken glass cut deep into her hands as she fought to steady herself. A voice roared above her. "Look at this mess. I can't even fix a simple supper anymore. I'm useless. Totally useless.''

The woman stormed out of the room, leaving obscenities dripping from the walls like the splattered cooking oil oozing from the broken bottle by the refrigerator.

Laura remained motionless. She heard the front door slam shut followed by a car engine shrieking to life. Spinning tires echoed down the long driveway and then, silence. The house was still. The only sound disturbing the evening calm was a girl's sobs.

* * *

Voyager rocked on its base as a cool wind whistled through the dark street. Occasionally a dog would bark in the distance, followed by a gruff voice ordering the animal to keep still. Jerusalem rested in the early morning calm.

Tony stood nearby, leaning against a wall. He was watching a group of men labor along the narrow street leading to the Temple courtyard. Their loud voices rang rough in the cool, damp air.

Inside the circle of men was a young woman, her face angry, frightened. The men shoved her along, demanding that she hurry. Every once in a while the woman would try to escape, but one of the men would grab her and yank her back in line.

After the group had passed Tony, the boy fell in behind them. The mob moved toward the tall white walls of the Temple glowing in the first rays of dawn.

Tony had decided to make this journey alone. Something he'd read in the Book the night before had raised questions in his mind. He wanted to see the event recorded there for himself.

In the Temple courtyard the group stopped in front of a large gathering of people who sat listening to a man reading from a scroll. Tony stood off to one side, waiting to see what would happen.

As the man looked up from his reading, Tony recognized him as the Nazarene.

"Rabbi," one from the group of men called out as he shoved the woman toward Jesus, "we've got a question for you."

The woman stood before the carpenter, cowering with fear.

Jesus studied the woman's face, then looked at the men. "Why do you treat this woman so roughly? What has she done to you?"

Several in the group reddened as their leader spoke. "We are not here to talk about us. This—this person was caught in the act of adultery."

The carpenter glanced at the woman. She did not lift her eyes.

The accuser continued. "In the law, Moses commanded us to stone such women. Now what do you say?"

Tony's mouth dropped open. It was a trick, an evil trick designed to force the Nazarene to choose between two laws: the law of God handed down centuries ago to the children of Israel in the desert, and the law of mercy that Jesus had been teaching.

If he said the woman should be stoned, he'd be turning his back on mercy. If he insisted that she shouldn't be stoned, the men who had brought her could accuse him of speaking against the law of God.

Tony's brow furrowed in confusion. The Ten Commandments, the rules and regulations written in the Book back at his workshop, were straight from God. Now God's Son was going around preaching mercy, about how we're supposed to help people, to love people, no matter what they've done. How could those two laws be followed at the same time?

Jesus turned toward the woman. Her face showed a look of hurt, embarrassment, shame.

Tony moved closer.

Quietly Jesus bent down on one knee. With his finger he began to write something in the loose sand covering the ground.

The mob became angry. "Hey, teacher," one of them

shouted, "where's all this great wisdom we've heard about? We've asked you a simple question and all you do is draw in the sand. Didn't your father teach you anything in that carpenter shop?"

The Nazarene stood. Turning to face the men, he spoke softly, firmly. "Let him who is without sin be the first to throw a stone at her." Stooping again, He continued writing in the sand.

"What's that supposed to mean?" one of the men shouted. "We're not the accused. She is!"

Suddenly an older member of the group lifted his hand. "Wait," he said. Moving to where Jesus was kneeling, he read the words scrawled in the sand. His face paled. Quickly he turned and left the gathering.

Another man stopped his taunting and read the words. Then he too quickly left.

One by one the men slipped away, until only the woman and Jesus remained.

The carpenter rose and looked around. "Where are the men who brought you here? Is there no one left to condemn you?"

The woman bowed her head, unable to look the Nazarene in the eye. "Only you are left," she said in a whisper.

"Then neither do I condemn you. Go. Sin no more."

The woman's eyes filled with tears as she gazed into the kind face of the teacher. She had been accused. She was guilty. But before this man, she had found something she had never known. In his eyes, in his voice, she had found acceptance, even in her sin. The law had condemned her, but the One who wrote the law had forgiven her.

Tony shook his head in amazement. The Nazarene had done it! This simple carpenter had faced the accusers and won.

As he made his way back to *Voyager,* Tony couldn't help smiling. He had seen the law of God in its true light. There was a place for mercy, for forgiveness.

In the distance he could see the men gathering once again. They were talking in whispers, pointing angrily toward the Temple. A frown shadowed Tony's face. He knew the Nazarene had not seen the last of that mob.

For the Love of Laura

MRS. PARKS was putting breakfast on the table as Tony entered the kitchen. Tie Li sat at her normal place, watching her mother spoon steaming mounds of scrambled eggs into a serving dish.

"Everything all right out in your workshop?" the woman asked, glancing at her son.

"Sure, Mom," Tony called over his shoulder as he headed for the refrigerator to get the milk. "Why do you ask?"

"Oh, I just saw some flashes of light out there and wondered if you were all right."

Tie Li looked up at her brother. "Why, Tony? Why you go to the workshop without me?"

Tony sat down beside his sister. "For your information, I just wanted to do something by myself. I'll tell you all about it later."

Tie Li nodded. "OK, Tony," she said. "But next time I go on the trip—I go with you to the workshop."

Tony glanced at Tie Li, then at his mother. "Sure, little sister. I won't forget."

"And the flashes of light?" Mrs. Parks pulled a pan of blueberry muffins from the oven. "What were they?"

Tony cleared his throat. "Sometimes my experiments get rather, uh, dramatic. I'll bet you thought aliens from another planet had landed. It was nothing as exciting as that."

"Just be careful out there," Mrs. Parks urged. "I don't want you doing anything dangerous."

"Don't worry, Mom," Tony soothed. "I won't burn down the barn, if that's what you mean."

Mrs. Parks settled in her chair and smiled over at her son. "Mothers just worry. I think it's in our job description."

Tony chuckled. "I'll be careful. I mean, hey, my computer is out there. You *know* I won't let anything bad happen to it!"

"Oh, yes," Mrs. Parks nodded, "your precious computer. Sorry. I forgot."

Kim and Mr. Parks sauntered into the room and pulled their chairs up to the table. Soon happy chatter warmed the country kitchen as hungry mouths enjoyed the early-morning feast Mrs. Parks had prepared.

Near the end of the meal a knock echoed from the front door. Tie Li slipped from her chair and trotted toward the hallway. "I'll get it," she called, her footsteps thumping on the wooden floorboards.

"I wonder who that could be?" Mrs. Parks said.

Tony took another bite of his muffin. "Probably some feed salesman. Do we need any?"

Mr. Parks shook his head. "I don't think so."

Tie Li returned on the run, deep concern showing in her eyes. "Tony, someone want to see you. Hurry!" She raced back to the door.

"What's the matter, Tie Li? Who is it?"

The little girl didn't respond. Tony got up and ran to the front hallway. He stopped when he saw a familiar form waiting by the door. His smile froze to horror when the visitor looked up at him.

"Laura!" Tony drew in a sharp breath. "Laura, what happened to your face?"

The girl began to cry.

"Mom, Dad, come quick!" Tony's voice was high, strained. "Something's happened to Laura."

Mr. Parks arrived just as the girl lost her ability to stand. He carried the cold, snow-covered bundle into the living room and placed her gently on the couch. Mrs. Parks stood in the doorway rapidly pressing numbers on the wall phone.

"Laura," Tony pleaded, "what happened? Who hurt you? Who did this to you?" The boy felt himself begin to cry, but he didn't care.

Laura's face was terribly swollen, one eye closed tightly. Bloodstains darkened her nose and chin.

Tony gasped when he saw the girl's hands. Deep cuts traced jagged patterns across her palms and fingers. Dark red stains soaked through the girl's jeans at the knees.

Laura looked up at her friend. A crooked smile inched painfully across her face when she saw his concern. "Hi, Tony," she whispered, her voice trembling with exhaustion. "I knew you'd help me. Just like you help Tie Li. I knew you would."

The girl relaxed, her breathing softening to a steady rhythm. The long night was over. Now she had someone to care for her. Now she could sleep.

In the distance, a siren's wail cut through the early-morning air.

* * *

In the weeks that followed, Laura's recovery was slow but steady. After a few days in the hospital, she was released into the loving attention of the Parks family.

Tony, Tie Li, and Kim all worked overtime making sure their guest was comfortable. Each afternoon Tony would race from the school bus, down the long driveway, across the barnyard, into the big yellow house, and up the stairs to Tie Li's room, shedding coat, gloves, boots, and scarf as he went.

Mrs. Parks would follow him up the stairs, her arms burdened with a growing pile of winter garments.

Laura's eyes would brighten whenever Tony entered the room. She reveled in his care, sitting quietly, propped up on her pillows, as he described his latest invention, showed off his school papers, and gave detailed explanations about why electricity can't shock you if you're wearing rubber boots, or how a robin knows when to fly north, or what makes snow melt at 33 degrees and not before.

"Tony," the girl would say after each presentation, "you're pretty smart for a guy." Then Tony would redden and shuffle his feet.

Tie Li, who was usually sitting nearby, would snicker. "If I tell Tony he's smart he doesn't get red, he just agree."

"I do not," Tony would deny, his face turning a darker shade of crimson.

Laura and Tie Li would laugh and reassure the boy that smart was fine with both sisters and friends.

Each evening before bedtime Kim would stop by to make sure the visitor had enough blankets for her bed. Being the tallest in the group, he could reach the pile of fluffy comforters hiding in the hall closet.

Week by week Laura grew stronger, aided by the

constant attention and healing love of the people in the big yellow house.

There were changes taking place beyond the lace-lined windows of her room too. The sun seemed to linger a little longer each day. Occasionally a breeze would blow from the south, carrying with it the welcome promise of spring.

Icicles lost their grip on the eaves and crashed to the ground. Between the house and the barn, muddy green patches appeared on the lawn where only drifts of snow had been. It seemed as if the whole world had tired of winter and now waited eagerly for the last snowflake to fall so life could begin again in the fields and pastures surrounding the farm.

"It's almost here!" Tony stood by the window one bright morning, watching lines of northbound Canada geese slide silently across the sky like soldiers returning from battle. "I've counted 14 robins, three bluebirds, and two house wrens already. In the pasture I saw a groundhog crawl out of his burrow, yawn, then sniff the air."

Tie Li and Laura looked up from the floor where a checkers game was in progress. "What's almost here?" Tie Li wanted to know.

"Spring! You know, flowers, leaves, birds building nests, all that neat stuff."

"I like spring," Tie Li said.

"How do you know?" Tony countered. "You've never seen one here in this country."

"Well, it sound nice. Besides, I'm ready to go swimming. You like swimming, Laura?"

The girl nodded. "I like the beach. My mother—" She hesitated, then continued. "My mother used to take me in the summer."

Tony sat down beside his sister and studied the checkerboard. "I'm really sorry about what happened," he said. "I don't know what I'd do if my mom—"

"You don't have to worry about that ever," Laura interrupted. "Your mom is . . . is different. She likes herself. You guys are important to her."

The girl sighed. "My mother worried about too many things. Stuff bothered her, really *bothered* her. I don't hate her or anything like that. I guess I just don't understand. Maybe I never will. I don't know."

Laura leaned back against the bed. "I wish I could talk to her, but they won't let me. She wasn't always like she is now. I like to remember her the way she was before. She's my mother. I still love her."

Tony was silent for a long moment. In the confusion and pain of what Laura had been through he hadn't given much thought to Mrs. Bates. But sitting before him was someone who had felt the brunt of the woman's rage, yet still cared for her.

The boy remembered the words of the Nazarene that cool morning in Jerusalem. He'd said, "Neither do I condemn you. Go. Sin no more."

Turning to his friend, Tony spoke quietly. "That's mercy, Laura. You have mercy for your mother."

The girl shrugged. "I guess so. I don't like what my mother did. She hurt me real bad, but I still love her."

Tie Li looked up at Tony. "That make the carpenter happy, huh?"

Laura glanced at Tie Li. "Carpenter? What carpenter?"

"It's a long story," Tony said, grinning at his sister. "We'll tell you about it someday."

Mrs. Parks appeared at the door of Tie Li's room. "Laura," she called, a smile spreading across her face, "you have a visitor."

"A visitor? Me?"

The children followed Mrs. Parks down the stairs and into the living room. Laura saw a figure standing by the window. "Did you want to see me?" she asked.

The visitor turned. "I've been waiting six years to see you, princess."

Tears stung the girl's eyes as she recognized the kind face from the picture. "Papa?" she cried, her voice filled with unbelief. "Papa, is that you?"

The man rushed across the room and engulfed the girl in his arms. His tears mingled with hers as he held her tightly, lost in the realization that their long separation had ended.

"Laura," he said when he was able to speak, "I didn't go away because I wanted to. Your mother made the courts believe things that weren't true about me. But now the judge understands. Mother needs special help. They're sending her to a place where she can learn to love herself again. She'll need our support—and our forgiveness, too. Do you understand?"

Laura nodded. She looked into the eyes of her father. "Papa, you won't go away again, will you?"

The man nestled the girl's face in his hands. In a voice trembling with emotion he said, "I will never leave you, Laura. You can count on it."

"Papa! Oh, Papa!" The words were choked, but the meaning was clear. In the life of Laura Bates, mercy had triumphed again.

The Father's Voice

IKNOW, I know." Tony typed furiously on his keyboard. "We haven't gone on a trip in *Voyager* for more than a month. Give me a break, you guys. I had other things on my mind."

"And we know what. Or should I say *who!*" Kim chided.

Tie Li giggled. "Can't you think of girl *and* something else?"

Tony stopped typing, sighed, then continued. "Will you quit bugging me?" he muttered. "Now that Laura's dad is taking care of her, we can get back to normal around here." Tony smiled. "She was pretty nice, though, wasn't she?"

Kim rolled his eyes. "Oh, brother! When Tony's in love, it's sickening."

"Well," Tony shot back, "listen to old Mr. Lonely Heart here. Didn't I see you drooling over Cindy Pareski the other day? You almost walked into a wall."

Kim blushed. "She's just a friend."

"Yeah, like Romeo was a friend to Juliet."

Tie Li covered her ears. "Girls, girls, girls! All you talk

131

about is girls. Why don't you talk about fun stuff?''

"Such as?'' Kim questioned.

"You know, stuff like swimming, chasing butterflies, making chocolate-chip cookies. *Eating* chocolate-chip cookies.''

Kim smiled. "Someday you'll understand.''

Tie Li shook her head. "Everybody tells me, 'Someday you'll understand.' But I'll never understand. Someday never come!''

"There,'' Tony called out, happy to change the subject. *"Voyager's* ready! We're heading for a village in Galilee, not far from Nazareth. The carpenter will be passing by there.''

Kim and Tie Li took their places in Tony's invention. The little girl tightened the chin strap of her football helmet and smiled up at her brother. "It's OK you like girls,'' she said shyly. "Just don't forget about me.''

Kim patted her on top of her helmet. "No chance of that, silly. You're still my *favorite* girl.''

Tie Li beamed. Even if she didn't understand boy-girl love, she did enjoy being Kim's sister. She liked the feeling of belonging it brought. Were other kinds of love like that too? Oh well, she'd find out someday. At least that's what everybody kept telling her.

Tony entered the machine and barked out his usual order. *"Voyager,* power up.'' The invention responded with flickering lights and glowing screens. Internal system motors hummed to life as each phase of the start-up sequence performed in rapid order.

With complex keyboard commands, Tony guided his machine through its long self-examination. Tie Li watched the on-board computer respond to Tony's checks and double-checks. Words flashed across the screen.

POWER—INTERNAL
SYSCONFIG—COMPLETE
POLARITY—RANSFERRED TO I/O
SEQUENCE COMMAND—ACTIVATED

Tony's hands flew between panels and switches, his eyes staring hard in concentration.

CLOCK—RUNNING
SIDE STEP—ON
TRANSLATOR CIRCUITS—ON STANDBY
STABILIZING ARM—FULL SWING
MASTER OVERRIDE—ARMED
POWER RESERVE—100 PERCENT
DESTINATION CODE—ENTERED AND CROSS-CHECKED
VOYAGER STANDING BY . . .

Tony looked at Kim, then at Tie Li. Each gave the thumbs-up signal. Turning to the panel above his head, the boy spoke firmly. *"Voyager, go!"*

The machine glowed blue, then white. With a roaring sound like a strong wind, *Voyager* faded from view.

Inside, Tony carefully monitored the illuminated dials circling the panel by his right arm. Words on the main screen reported the children's progress back through the centuries.

CONDITION—NORMAL   VOYAGER   UNDER WAY
POWER FLOW—CONSTANT
TIME-WALL INSERTION IN—4, 3, 2, 1.

Voyager jolted hard as the machine slammed against the electrical barrier maintaining the normal sequence of time. The children felt the boundary give way as Tony's invention continued its journey.

Soon *Voyager's* swaying motion lessened. Then, with a

slight bump, it stopped altogether.

"We're here," Tony breathed. "Some ride, huh?"

Kim let out a nervous sigh. "It doesn't get any easier. Someday we're going to all end up nowhere, no time, with no way back."

"Now there's an interesting theory." Tony rubbed his chin thoughtfully.

"Never mind," Kim urged. "Let's not experiment."

Tony laughed. "Don't worry. I'll take good care of you."

The three placed the plastic sheet over *Voyager,* and Tony checked the solar recharge switch. With everything in order, the children set out to explore the landing site.

The machine had settled on the summit of a small hill. Farmers' fields, burdened with ripening grain, spread out toward the horizon. Carpets of wheat lay in neat golden squares. The fields were crisscrossed by rows of trees and an occasional splash of wildflowers.

At the base of the hill, a small village lined with low, whitewashed houses basked in the hot midday sun. Occasionally a distant bird would call out in defense of its territory, but after its shrill voice echoed into silence, the hillside was still once again. Far to the east, the blue waters of Galilee sparkled diamond-like in the yellow palm of the land.

"There's something to be said about the past," Kim said, his eyes drinking in the scenic beauty. "No factories, no cars, no airplanes. Everything seems . . . natural, peaceful."

"You're right." Tony drew in a deep breath of the nature-scented air. "I love the country. I guess the Nazarene liked it too. The Book says he spent a lot of time up here."

Tie Li lifted her hand. "Hey, I think I hear talking."

Over the rise, not far from where the children stood, a group of men approached. Jesus was in the lead. The conversation sounded heated.

"You've got everyone confused," one of the men was saying. "Some are calling you Elijah, some say you're the prophet Jeremiah. I even heard one guy say he thought you were your cousin John the Baptist!"

The group paused on the hilltop. "So why don't you just tell people who *you* are?"

The carpenter turned to his followers. He studied each face as if searching for something. In a quiet, almost sad voice he said, "Whom do *you* say that I am?"

No one spoke. A gentle breeze moved through the grasses covering the hillside. Some in the group shuffled their feet nervously. Throats cleared. A man coughed. Deep silence hung heavy over the gathering.

The Carpenter nodded slowly, his eyes still searching the faces before him.

Suddenly a deep, penetrating voice called out, "You are Christ, the Son of the living God!"

Simon Peter stepped from behind the group and stood before Jesus. "The Son of God. That's who You are."

The Nazarene smiled. His face radiated a renewed hope, a growing resolution. It seemed as if he'd drawn strength from the fisherman's words.

"Simon Peter," Jesus said, "no person told you that I was the Son of God. My Father placed that truth in your heart, and you believed."

Turning again to his followers, Jesus continued. "This is the kind of faith that will be the cornerstone of my church, and even death will not destroy it. With the power generated by simple faith, you can do *anything*. Heaven will stand by your side. Please, listen to my Father when He speaks to you.''

Peter's brother, Andrew, moved to the front of the group. ''Master, how will we know?'' he asked. ''What does the Father's voice sound like?''

Jesus pointed down the hill. ''Come. I'll show you.''

Tony, Tie Li, and Kim followed the group along the road leading to the village. At the edge of town, dogs barked their warnings, then took shelter inside the simple structures lining the narrow streets.

Jesus paused by the well that had been dug in the center of the village. ''Listen,'' he said, raising his hand. ''Listen very carefully, and you will hear my Father's voice.''

Silence fell over the gathering as every ear strained to hear what the Carpenter had promised. At first there was nothing, then from down one of the streets came a muffled sob. A woman was crying softly to herself.

From another corner of the village, a moan lifted from a bed of sickness and drifted through the open door of a house.

Angry voices echoed from yet another direction as a distant argument punctuated the afternoon stillness.

''Do you hear it?'' the Carpenter asked. ''Do you hear my Father's voice?''

Andrew stepped forward and stood beside Jesus. ''Master,'' he said quietly, ''there are only the sounds of the village reaching our ears. We hear no voice from heaven.''

Jesus motioned for the group to follow. He led them down the street in the direction of the soft sobs. Pausing at a door, he called out, ''Woman, why do you weep?''

A gaunt, tear-stained face emerged from the darkness of the house. ''My son,'' the woman cried, ''is unable to walk. An accident struck him down. Now the crops wait in the fields, and he can't bring in the harvest.''

A young man hobbled to the door, his leg wrapped in strips of cloth. He leaned heavily on a rough wooden cane. ''Sir,'' he pleaded, ''help us. We have no one.''

''Oh, but you do,'' Jesus countered. ''You have the Father. He has heard your cry. Go. The harvest waits for you.''

The young man looked at his mother, then back at the stranger standing by the door. The cane dropped from his hand as he took a faltering step forward. The leg supported him.

A look of wonder spread across the young man's face. ''My leg,'' he called out. ''My leg is healed! My leg is healed!''

Slowly, then with increasing confidence he moved about the room. ''Mother,'' he cried, ''look! I'm walking. Do you see me? I'm walking!'' He turned back toward the door, but the stranger was gone.

Jesus paused at another house. Inside, moans of sickness hung heavy in the damp air. He told his followers to wait outside as he stepped into the dwelling. Within minutes, the moans had stopped. In their place were joyous shouts.

At house after house the carpenter paused, turning sorrow to joy, sickness to healing, anger to peace.

At the edge of the village he turned and looked back along the dusty streets. ''Listen again,'' he said. This time there were no moans, no angry shouts, no crying. The only sounds were those of praise and thanksgiving.

Jesus smiled. ''The voice of God can be heard any place there is sorrow, pain, and anger. When you touch another human life, you're answering the call of my Father. Listen for it. His voice is everywhere.''

The group moved down the road away from the village, toward the distant waters of Galilee. Behind them a town basked in the heat of the noonday sun—and reveled in the warmth of the Master's touch.

Enough

"YOU'RE very quiet today." Dr. McFerren tapped his pencil on the desktop. "I've been doing most of the talking. Are you feeling all right?"

Kim stirred. "What's that, Dr. McFerren? Did you say something?"

The psychiatrist laughed out loud. "Apparently nothing important."

"Oh," Kim blushed. "I'm sorry. I guess I'm not a very good patient today."

The man rose and walked over to where Kim was sitting. Pulling up a chair, he sat down and studied the boy's face. "What's the matter? You seem a million miles away."

"I am, sort of," Kim admitted. "I was thinking about something I saw . . . uh . . . read last week."

"You want to tell me about it?"

The boy nodded. "I do, but I don't know how. You see, it has to do with religion and stuff like that."

Dr. McFerren smiled. "That's OK. I can take it."

"That's not what I mean," Kim said. "Religion, God,

this is all new to me. Sometimes it's hard to understand what's going on. I mean, you say there's a God, but you don't really like Him. But God is kind and loving. How can you not like a God who does good things for people?"

"Kim, it's not what God does that I don't like. It's what He *doesn't* do."

"What do you mean?"

Dr. McFerren thought for a minute. "I just wish He'd . . . help people more. There's so much pain and violence around these days. Why doesn't this all-powerful God step in and stop it?"

"But He did step in," Kim countered. "I saw . . . I mean, I read where His Son Jesus was born on this earth and grew up to be a kind and loving man. He used His power to make sick people well and sad people happy. He's been here, doing just what you said. Yet few people believed in Him or trusted Him then. It's the same today. Why is that?"

The man studied Kim's face. "You're serious about this, aren't you? I mean, this is important to you."

"Well, yes," Kim nodded. "I want to know what I'm supposed to do with God."

"You're asking the wrong man," Dr. McFerren said coldly.

"No, I don't think so. You said you went to church when you were a little boy. You prayed. You sang songs and listened to sermons. You must have believed in Him then."

The doctor leaned back in his chair. "I was just a boy. I grew up."

"But doesn't God grow up too?"

Dr. McFerren sat in silence for a long moment. Slowly he rose to his feet and walked to the window. "You know

140

what happened," he said quietly. "You remember I told you about my father."

"Hey, I lost my father too," Kim said. "And my mother. Was that God's fault?"

"*Yes!*" The doctor whirled and faced the boy. "Yes! He could have stopped it. He could have kept it from happening. But He didn't. He just sat there and did nothing—"

"Dr. McFerren," Kim interrupted, "the God I'm learning about would never just sit and let something bad happen if He could stop it. He's kind, loving. He heals sicknesses, makes crippled people walk again. He cries when people cry. Laughs when they laugh. But even with Him standing right there, bad things continued to happen all around, in the next village, the next town."

"Jesus was human," the doctor argued. "God the Father is divine. He's not limited like His Son was."

"I'm sorry, but I don't agree, Dr. McFerren. Jesus didn't seem to be limited at all. But He only used His power on those who wanted it, who had faith in it."

The man's face reddened. "So you're saying my father died because I didn't have faith in God?"

"Oh, no! Please don't think I meant that at all!" Kim sat back heavily in his chair. "There, you see, I get to a certain point and then nothing makes sense anymore. Don't be angry with me. I'm confused too."

The doctor's face softened as he returned to the chair beside Kim. "Forgive me. I didn't mean to raise my voice at you. I guess this is a touchy subject for both of us."

Kim nodded. "The answer seems so close. I just want to reach out and grab it so I can understand."

"Maybe," the doctor said quietly, "maybe there is no answer to all this. Maybe we're not supposed to understand. On one hand we have a God who loves us. On the other hand we have pain and suffering. Yet when Jesus lived on this earth, He suffered and felt pain. He didn't even try to stay out of it. He could have, but He didn't. It was as if . . . He . . .''

The man leaned back against his chair, his eyes closed. "O God," he whispered, "forgive me."

Kim drew in a sharp breath. "Dr. McFerren, what's the matter?"

The man shook his head slowly from side to side. "I've been such a fool. For so long I've been blaming God for my father's death, as if He were treating me worse than He treats other people. But Kim, God didn't stop evil from hurting His own Son. Yet Jesus never questioned, never blamed, never turned against His Father. He just obeyed.

"Don't you see? There must be a reason that God doesn't step in and stop sin and evil in this world. And whatever the reason, it was good enough for Jesus. He lived and died to support it."

The man walked back to the window. "It's like my daddy used to say when I'd complain about our lot in life. He'd look me right in the eye and say, 'Son, don't ask why. Just hang in there. The good Lord knows what's going on. He'll fix it in the end.' And you know, He has fixed it so many times. I've just been so blinded by my own disappointments I didn't take the time to see." The man turned and faced Kim. "We may not like what's going on, but God will have the last word. Jesus must have known that deep down in His heart."

Kim nodded slowly. "Recently I heard someone say 'God's voice is everywhere.' Maybe some people hear it best when they're hurting."

"Yeah, I guess you're right." The doctor smiled. "But there's got to be an easier way."

A tiny "beep" sounded from the man's arm. Glancing at his watch, Dr. McFerren sighed. "I'm afraid our time is up. I've got another patient waiting. I appreciate your honesty, Kim. Really."

The boy rose to leave. "Dr. McFerren, do you think we'll ever understand about God?"

"Probably not," the man said. "I guess He understands us. Maybe that's enough."

With a wave, Kim was gone. The doctor sat down behind his desk and leaned back into the soft arms of his chair. He closed his eyes. "Maybe that's enough," he repeated.

* * *

The cabin buzzed with activity as busy hands swarmed about the curtains, throw rugs, chairs, sofa, and linen closet. Spring cleaning had come to the little dwelling in the clearing in the woods.

Tony splashed a soapy concoction of his own invention on each windowpane and washed them till they seemed to disappear from view.

Kim crawled around on his hands and knees making sure all hidden deposits of dust and grime ceased to exist under the relentless attack of his foaming scrub brush.

In the kitchen Tie Li carefully dried the dishes Grandmother Parks handed her. She stopped to admire the colorful patterns etched in each plate and platter.

"This very pretty," she said, holding a serving dish up to the light streaming through a nearby Tony-washed window. "It remind me of flower garden."

"It is lovely, isn't it?" Grandmother agreed. "My mother gave that set to me."

"Oh," Tie Li gasped, "it must be very, very old."

"Well, Noah didn't use them in the ark, if that's what you mean."

Tie Li giggled. "There was no room in the ark for dishes. Just people and animals."

Tony called from a corner of the cabin. "What's it like being old, Grandmother?"

The woman sighed. "For one thing, everyone thinks you're older than you really are. For another thing, all children under 15 think you used to date Jonah."

"Oh," Tony said seriously, "you must have had a whale of a time."

The cabin erupted with laughter as Grandmother threw a bubbly dishrag across the room. It hit Tony squarely in the face.

Kim doubled over, his stomach aching with glee. "Look," he shouted, "Grandmother is spring-cleaning Tony!"

Tie Li slipped to the floor, her legs no longer able to support her shaking body. "I think he need more soap," she screeched.

Grandmother stumbled across the room, holding her sides. "Well, well," she mused, standing before her dishrag-crowned grandson. "Where should I start? Behind the ears, I think."

Tony wrapped his arms around the woman. "Grandmother," he cried, his face covered with suds, "you're the best, the very best, even if you are old enough to be a California redwood."

Renewed gales of laughter sprang through the cabin windows and drifted with the wind over the pasture and echoed deep in the forest. In every corner of the Parkses' farm, a new life was beginning for each tree and shrub. Animals scurried about, reveling in the newfound warmth.

The seasons were changing. Winter was fading away. Soon there'd be young ones to care for, mouths to feed, homes to protect. As with nature and humans alike, the Creator had made provision for new life.

But Tony, Tie Li, and Kim had more lessons to learn. In the weeks to come, they'd discover that sometimes new life comes at a terrible price.

Forgiving Love

AGRINDING, rattling noise interrupted the afternoon stillness surrounding the big yellow house. Tony glanced up from his homework.

"What on earth was that?" he muttered.

He listened, straining to hear more, but the only sound coming through his open window was the warbling work song of a busy house wren gathering twigs for his fence-post estate.

"*S-c-r-e-e-c-h... Bang!* There it was again. The boy got up from his desk and walked across the room. Bending low by the window, he searched the yard for the source of such an awful racket.

Ra-tat-tat-tat-boom-tinkle-thud! This was getting interesting. Then Tony stiffened as he realized the clamor was coming from the direction of his workshop.

"Hey," he yelled out from his second-story perch, "what's going on down there? Is there someone in my worksh—"

Crash! Tony jumped back from the window, almost tripping over the end of his bed. He raced down the stairs, through the kitchen, and out the back door. Running across the yard toward the barn, he envisioned his precious workshop in shambles, victim of some uninvited burglar or vandal. "Not *Voyager,*" he whispered to himself. "Please, not *Voyager.*"

The door to the workshop hung open. Tony entered, ready to do battle with whoever was causing the disturbance. The room was empty. But someone, or something, had been there just moments before. Tools, charts, print-outs, circuit boards, and computer cables lay in scattered heaps on the floor. Across his normally neat worktable, an assortment of books, electronic diagrams, software manuals, and drafting pencils created a frantic mosaic of destruction.

"Oh, help!" Tony gasped, his brain refusing to accept what his eyes were showing him.

Footsteps sounded in the doorway as Tie Li rushed into the room. "Tony, I saw you running. What the mat—" Her words caught in her throat. The girl surveyed the awful scene, her eyes wide with shock. "Tony!" she said breathlessly. "Your workshop. It look like war."

The boy nodded. "That's for sure."

"But who do this? Who make such a mess?"

Tony sighed. "I don't know, little sister. I just don't know."

"Can you fix it?"

"I think so." Tony stepped over a pile of broken glass that up until a few minutes ago had been a lamp. "It looks like my stuff was just thrown around the room. I don't see any major damage."

He flipped on his computer resting on one corner of the workbench. Tony studied the words and numbers appearing in rapid sequence across the screen.

Tie Li joined her brother at the keyboard. "Is *Voyager* OK?"

Tony typed the command **VOYAGER SYSCHK** and waited, watching the computer screen. Within moments the words **SYSCHK COMPLETE—ALL SYSTEMS NORMAL** flashed in glowing letters.

"Well, there doesn't seem to be anything wrong with the machine, but I'll run several more tests just in case." The boy scratched his head. "But I sure would like to know what happened in here."

Outside, a car door slammed and Kim's voice called out, "Tony, Tie Li, anybody home?"

"We in workshop," Tie Li shouted back, not looking up from the computer. Tony typed in command after command. Each time the screen reported everything normal.

Kim entered the room. "Whoa, what happened in here?"

"That's what we'd like to know," Tony said, his eyes concentrating on the words flashing in front of him.

"Is *Voyager* OK?"

"I guess so." The younger boy rested his arms on the workbench. "I don't understand. Nothing is stolen. No major damage has been done. My workshop's just been . . . trashed."

"I sorry, Tony." Tie Li placed her hand on her brother's shoulder. "I sorry this happened."

"One of life's little mysteries," Kim said soberly. "Kinda spooky."

"Yeah, spooky," Tony repeated.

Tie Li looked around the room. "I don't like spooky."

The three of them spent the remainder of the afternoon putting the workshop back in order. Tony's appraisal of the situation proved correct. Nothing was stolen. Whatever had paid a visit to the little room at the edge of the barn had simply rearranged its contents.

After the supper dishes had been washed and dried, the children excused themselves and made their way back to the workshop. Tony had promised another trip in payment for the hard work his brother and sister had provided all afternoon.

"We're going to Galilee," he said, booting up his computer. "The Book says the Nazarene spent a lot of time there."

"I don't blame Him," Kim added. "It's beautiful along the shoreline, especially in the early morning, like when we were there last time."

"Everybody is probably happy that Jesus is God's Son," Tie Lie joined in. "I know it make *me* happy to know that."

Tony paused, a puzzled look on his face. "You'd think so, wouldn't you? But the Book says not very many people believed who He was. Most just ignored him. Strange, isn't it?"

Kim and Tie Li nodded. "He just wanted to help them," the older boy said thoughtfully. "It is strange."

Tony motioned for the others to take their places in his machine. Soon the workshop sat empty. *Voyager* was underway.

As usual, the machine materialized right where Tony had programmed it to appear. The Sea of Galilee sparkled in the noonday sun, its silver waves washing along the sandy shore stretching in a wide arc in both directions. Noisy gulls fought for fish scraps among abandoned boats. Cool sea breezes carried the sweet scent of distant fruit orchards and freshly plowed fields out over the waters where fish jumped at low-flying insects. The sun felt warm and friendly on the faces of the young visitors.

"Like I said, this is a great place." Kim skipped a stone across the waves. "Everybody should have a Galilee to go to."

"Even kids like us?" Tony pointed north along the shoreline.

The children saw a boy about their own age walking with determined steps along the beach. He carried a small bundle thrown over his shoulder. The young traveler didn't notice the sparkling water's cool breezes or the distant mountains. He walked, head down, mumbling to himself. As he approached, it became evident he'd been crying.

"Some friend," the boy said, kicking at a stone in the sand, almost tripping himself in the process. "Herod should have such a friend."

When he reached a fishing boat resting on the sands near where the children stood, the boy stopped, letting his load drop to the ground. "What's the use?" he called out to no one. "You do your best, and nobody notices. You make one little mistake, and the whole world knows all about it." He turned and faced the gentle waves washing in from the deep-blue surface of Galilee. "Fish," he shouted into the wind, "you've got it made. Nobody tells you what to do. Nobody sits around waiting for you to make a mistake. Nobody yells at you when you do something wrong."

"Yes, but who wants to be a fish?" A man's voice echoed along the shore. Startled, the boy looked up to see a traveler coming down the hillside toward the waters.

"It's Jesus," Tie Li whispered.

The man walked over to where the young boy stood. "You look angry," he said.

"What do you care?" the boy snapped back. "You're just like everybody else."

"Maybe."

"Oh, I suppose you've never had your best friend turn on you like a jackal."

The man paused. He looked out over the waters, his face suddenly sad. "Everybody has a friend like that sometime in his life. It's just . . . part of living in a sinful world." He turned back toward the boy. "It must have happened to you a little earlier than some. You want to tell me about it?"

The boy studied the Man's face. "I know you. You're that rabbi my village is talking about. I saw you not long ago over there on the hillside. Yes . . . I remember. You talked about peacemakers and love and stuff like that."

"I'm glad you were listening."

"Hey, you're a pretty good storyteller."

"Thank you."

The boy looked out over the waves. "How come nobody does what you said?"

"I wish I knew." The Nazarene sat down on the sand. "It would make life a lot easier on all of us."

The boy thought for a moment. "Rabbi, you said for us to love our enemies. But what if our enemy used to be our best friend? What if he hurt us real bad? It's hard to love someone all over again."

The Nazarene nodded. "Yes, it is hard. You feel . . . betrayed, right?"

"Yeah, that's it. How do you love a friend who betrayed you?"

The young boy sat down in the sand beside the man. He waited, watching the waves spread across the shore.

"It depends on what kind of love you had for your friend in the first place," the man said thoughtfully.

"What *kind* of love?" The boy looked up in surprise. "I thought there was only one kind."

"Oh, there are many types of love, but only a few include forgiveness. You see, that's the secret. The best love is forgiving love. That means you make a person your friend, no matter what he or she does in the future. You say, 'I will be this person's friend no matter what happens.' Then, when your buddy does something to hurt you, you have forgiveness all ready and waiting. You may have to work at it, but it's the best way to love someone." The man's voice softened. "Believe me, sometimes it's the *only* way that love is possible."

"Forgiving love," the boy repeated. "Do you love all your friends that way?"

The Nazarene smiled, but the boy noticed tears in the eyes of the traveler. "Yes, I do," he said softly. "I must."

"There you are!" A group of disciples joined the two on the shore. "We've been looking for you. Let's get going. They're expecting us for supper."

The Nazarene stood and helped the boy to his feet. "Would you like to walk with us? We're heading north to Capernaum. Is that where you are going?"

The young boy thought for a moment. "Yeah, that's where I'm going. That's where I live."

Jesus smiled and nodded. "Good. Walk with us."

One of the disciples pulled the Rabbi aside. "Master, we don't have time to baby-sit a runaway kid. You know that's what he is, don't you? I mean, look at his bundle. Classic runaway, if you ask me."

"Yes, I know," the Rabbi said. "But he needs a friend right now. You can understand that, can't you, Judas?"

The group walked away, moving along the shoreline. Tony, Kim, and Tie Li watched them go, each lost in thought. The Nazarene had presented a new meaning for love. It was simple, beautiful. Tony frowned. Time would tell just how strong forgiving love can be.

Rebound

VOYAGER moved through the centuries like a shadow passing quickly over the face of time. For the children huddled inside the wooden confines of Tony's machine, the journey was one of vibrations, high-pitched windlike sounds, and swaying sensations.

As usual, Tony's eyes remained fixed on the flickering screens lining the panel above his head. His hands moved in complex rhythms, entering commands, flipping switches, pressing buttons. The boy's mind worked in exact harmony with the electronic surges pulsing through the wire and microprocessor-packed brain of *Voyager's* internal computer systems. It was as if he and the machine were one intelligent being, slipping through the magnetic and gravitational boundaries that held time in its orderly flow toward the future.

Kim watched in quiet confusion. Nothing in his past related to the fantastic realities he was experiencing. His life was now far removed from the simple existence he'd grown accustomed to at the edge of the jungle. The changes were more than he'd ever imagined possible.

He had met a man, a kind, loving man, who understood the pain of losing and the hidden fear of loneliness. The Nazarene seemed to have the ability to see beyond the surface of a person's life. He seemed to know the very thoughts of those whom he met.

Kim smiled in the dim-lit atmosphere of *Voyager*. This Jesus could understand his deepest thoughts. This simple carpenter from Nazareth had the power to do more than any doctor or psychiatrist could ever hope to, because he understood people from the inside out.

The boy glanced down at his sister. Her helmeted head moved back and forth, swaying with the constant motion of Tony's invention. Kim nodded to himself. Only a good God, only a Being who understood the human heart, could create the love he felt for this little girl. This type of emotion was no accident of nature. Love was a planned by-product of God's creative power. The man on the shore understood its awesome potential. Those he touched soon learned of it too.

Kim noticed Tony's movements had become quicker, more aggravated. His brother's hand would reach for a switch, hesitate, then change course and quickly rotate a knob or enter a command hurriedly on the keyboard.

Kim cleared his throat. "Is everything all right?" he called above the noise.

Tony didn't answer. His movements became even more sporadic, uncertain, as if he wasn't sure of what to do.

"Tony? What's the matter?"

"Look at this," Tony called out, his finger pointing at the main system screen. Kim saw words glowing there that he'd never seen before. **WARNING: TIME FLOW AL-TERED—CORRECT IMMEDIATELY!** Tony typed furiously. The older boy noticed sweat running down the side of his brother's face.

WARNING: TIME FLOW ALTERED—COR-RECT IMMEDIATELY!

Tony banged his fist on a panel. The screen continued to flash its solemn message. **WARNING: TIME FLOW ALTERED—CORRECT IMMEDIATELY!**

"I'm trying! I'm trying!" Tony shouted at the persistent screen.

Tie Li looked up at her brothers. "What happening?" she asked, her voice lost in the increasing noise building around the travelers.

"Something's not right here," Tony shouted, his voice thin, high.

The screen flashed another message: **TIME FLOW OUT OF PHASE—CHECK POLARITY!**

"I did! I did!" Tony toggled a series of switches. Nothing changed. Kim noticed fear in his brother's eyes.

Then . . . **SEQUENCE LOST—SEQUENCE LOST —SEQUENCE LOST—PREPARE FOR REBOUND!**

"No!" Tony screamed.

REBOUND IN: 5-4 . . .

"Kim, Tie Li, *hold on!*" Tony's face was suddenly ashen . . . **3-2 . . .**

An alarm sounded somewhere inside *Voyager* as the countdown continued. . . . **1—REBOUND COM-MENCED!**

The children slammed hard against one side of *Voyager* as the machine seemed to turn sharply. Sparks ignited and arched from the crevasses above their heads, showering hot, glowing traces of burning wiring and insulation down on them.

Kim saw the wooden slats by his arm twist and pull

apart. Outside, streams of green and yellow light sped by, like flashes from a laser gun. He called out, but his voice sounded like a whisper compared to the piercing sounds pressing against his ears.

Tony held Tie Li tightly against his waist, his eyes closed.

Voyager strained at every nut and bolt, nail and hinge. Tony realized that if the torture continued, the machine would break up completely. The forces coming to bear on the fragile structure seemed bent on destroying it and its contents.

"Tony? What happening? What happening?" Tie Li glanced about wide-eyed as the box lurched from side to side.

"We've changed course in time!" Tony shouted. "I don't believe this." He pointed again at the screen. *"Voyager* is accelerating in reverse. We're not heading into the future. We're . . . we're heading into the past! Into . . . prehistory!"

"Do something, Tony," Kim encouraged, his throat tight with fear. "Do something quick!"

"I can't! We're out of control. *Voyager* is doing the best it can with what it knows. We're in a time-form I haven't programmed for. *Voyager* will have to work this one out all by itself. This is beyond me."

Suddenly Tony shouted, "Wait!" and began typing. "I remember creating a cease command after Simon Gorby tried to get himself killed in this thing last fall. It just might work!"

"Then do it, Tony. *Do it!*" Kim's voice was shaking.

Tony typed as quickly as his frightened fingers would allow.

VOYAGER: 3Q34OUTIMEPASS SYSTEM CEASE —NOW.

The machine answered immediately: **CEASE COMMAND REQUESTED—OPERATOR CONFIRM . . . Y/N**

Tony pressed the Y key. The screen went blank. Then **. . . CEASE SEQUENCE UNDER WAY—PREPARE FOR SHUTDOWN.**

"All right!" Tony yelled. "Hold on, you guys. Hold on!"

Voyager tilted hard to the right. The children felt themselves falling, turning, spinning. The noise changed from a high-pitched scream to a low growl. Then, with a sudden jolt, everything was quiet.

No one moved. The only sound was the stabilizing arm slowly spinning down. The screen flashed another message: **WARNING—CEASE SEQUENCE COMPLETED —CHECK ALL SYSTEMS BEFORE PROCEEDING—VOYAGER STANDING BY.**

Tony let out a long sigh. "You guys OK?" he asked in a voice not much above a whisper.

Kim nodded. Tie Li drew in a shaky breath. "I OK."

The younger boy leaned his head against a panel. "I don't understand. It's as if someone messed with my internal programming. *Voyager* shouldn't have gotten off course like this. It just shouldn't have happened."

Kim glanced over at his brother. "The intruder—the one who messed up your workshop—could he have done it? Could he have made this happen?"

Tony nodded slowly. "Yes, if he knew what he was doing, he could have. But no one knows *Voyager* like I do. No one."

The three stood in silence. Was this possible? Did

158

someone purposely try to sabotage the machine? Tony shook his head as if to throw off such an awful thought. "Whatever the reason, we're here, and I've got to get us back. You guys hang in there. I'll see what I can do."

The computerized conversation between inventor and machine was quick and to the point:

VOYAGER: STATUS CHECK?
SYSTEMS OPERATIONAL—SOME MARGINAL DAMAGE REPORT?
STANDBY, CHECKING: STABILIZING ARM—25 PERCENT SPIN CAPABLE
TIMEWALL INSERTER—MARGINAL
TIME FLOW—MARGINAL
POLARITY—NEGATIVE (OPERATOR ALTERED)
CLOCK-MARGINAL POWER RESERVE—5 PERCENT (DRAIN: HIGH)

Tony grimaced. "Now for the important one." He carefully typed a command on the keyboard.

RETURN POSSIBLE?

The screen went blank for what seemed like hours, though it was just a matter of seconds. Then words appeared.

RETURN POSSIBLE—45 PERCENT CHANCE OF SURVIVAL—ENTER INTENTIONS . . .

"Oh, that's just great," Tony sighed. "Forty-five percent."

"But we've got to get back. We've got to try," Kim urged.

Tony nodded. "You guys relax. This could take a while."

Kim reached up to unlatch the door. "We'll be outside."

"Wait!" Tony warned. "There's something I need to tell you. You're not going to find much out there."

"Why?"

"Well, we're not exactly at a time when there was much around."

"What time is it?"

Tony pointed at a screen above his head. Kim read the words glowing at the bottom left-hand corner: **YEAR: 2.35 MILLION B.C.**

"Two million years ago!" Kim cried out in astonishment. "We're 2 million years before Christ!"

"I'm afraid so."

"Then there'll be dinosaurs and cavemen and strange creatures out there!"

Tony shrugged. "That's what some people say. I just wanted to warn you."

Tie Li grabbed hold of Kim's leg. "I scared. Take me home to big yellow house *right now!*"

"I'm working on it," Tony encouraged. *"Voyager* can support us here for"—he entered a command on the keyboard and studied the screen—"thirty-seven minutes. If we're not out by then . . . we live here."

"What a soothing thought," Kim groaned. "Come on, Tie Li. We've got to let Tony work."

The older boy unlatched the door. "Whatever's out there is about to have some visitors," he announced.

The Void

MR. PARKS slid the large, heavy door along its metal track until it clanked tightly against the far wall of the barn, sealing the cows in their comfortable pens for the night. The milking was done, fresh water rippled in the long troughs lining the large feeding area, and the sound of soft munching told the weary farmer his four-legged charges were happily chewing their cuds.

The man let out a satisfied sigh. Soon his cows could roam the pastures beyond the barnyard, grazing contentedly on the new spring grasses growing higher and greener with each passing day.

His stockpile of feed was getting low, but it would last. He had harvested just enough corn and oats the previous year to see his herd through the long winter months.

Walking toward the house, he noticed that the light in Tony's workshop was still on. It was unusual for the children to be out so late in the evening, especially on a school night. Changing course, he headed back toward the barn. Inside he would find no children, and most puzzling of all, no *Voyager*.

As the farmer's hand reached out to open the door of the workshop he heard his name.

"Bob? Bob. Telephone!" Mrs. Parks stood on the back porch of the big yellow house calling into the evening shadows. "It's your mother."

The man hesitated, his hand resting on the doorknob. He heard nothing inside. The children must be concentrating on something important. Turning, he resumed his journey toward the house. "I'm coming," he called. "Tell her I'll be right there." He'd check on the children later.

* * *

Kim squared his shoulders, trying to look brave. "You ready?" he asked.

Tie Li swallowed hard. "I ready."

The door to *Voyager* opened slowly. Eager eyes appeared as the hinges creaked their own uncertainty. Tie Li held her breath. She had heard stories and seen pictures of what the world was supposed to have looked like millions of years ago. Now she'd see for herself.

An eerie blackness surrounded the machine. Kim and Tie Li stood in the doorway, holding each other, waiting for the inevitable scream of some prehistoric beast to cut through the silence.

"It must be night here," Kim whispered. "I can't see anything."

"Nope," Tony said, his eyes searching the screens. "*Voyager* reports it's two o'clock in the afternoon."

"What?" Kim turned to face his brother. "Two o'clock . . . in the afternoon? Where's the sun?"

Tie Li started to step down from *Voyager* but jerked her foot back, her face suddenly pale. "Wh—wh—where the ground? There no ground!" Kim gazed into the blackness. "Hey," he said, his voice startled, confused, "there's

162

nothing out there! I mean nothing. No light, no ground, no animals, nothing!''

Kim and Tie Li both turned to face Tony. The boy continued his work. ''Tony?'' Kim's voice sounded a little irritated. ''Tony! What's going on? Where is everything?''

''Everything's out there. It's just not put together yet.''

''Put together? What do you mean 'put together'? And if you're so smart, tell me this. If there's no ground out there, what is this box of yours sitting on, thin air?''

Tony smiled. ''Sort of.''

''Come on Tony,'' Kim urged, his voice rising a little. ''What's going on?''

''OK, OK,'' the younger boy sighed, a twinkle in his eye. ''If you must know.''

Tie Li nodded. ''Oh, we must, we must.''

''I'll answer your last question first. *Voyager* is sitting on about 4,000 volts of electricity. We're suspended between three waypoints in time—the time it is back home on the farm, the time it was in Galilee, and the amount of time that passed during our little rebound experience. Each time exists, although not at the same instant. You see, *Voyager* locks onto three moments in history, generates a new time-flow structure from that information, and then creates a three-dimensional overlay of whatever date and hour I choose. Then it's a simple matter of slipping into the new generated time-flow, and going there. See?''

Kim's mouth hung open as he nodded slowly. ''Sorry I asked.''

''But why there nothing outside?'' Tie Li urged.

''Well, Creation hasn't happened yet,'' Tony said, turning a knob above his head.

''Creation?'' Kim interrupted. ''You mean the creation

of the world? I remember you telling me about that back in the cabin.''

The boy glanced out the door, then back at his brother. ''But the dinosaurs, the flying reptiles, the monkeys, where are they? They did exist didn't they?''

''Oh yes,'' Tony nodded, ''they certainly did, but not before Creation. They were . . . like . . . mutants that came from the beautiful creatures God formed. Of course, when He made the animals at Creation, they didn't go around eating each other. All that stuff came later as a result of sin.''

''Does the Book in your workshop talk about this?'' Kim asked, pointing out into the blackness.

''Right at the very beginning. It says the world was without form, and void, and darkness was on the face of the deep. I believe that describes what you see out there pretty good.''

''It's a void, all right,'' Kim agreed. ''There's just . . . nothing out there. But the scientists say—''

''I know what the scientists say,'' Tony interrupted. ''But they're wrong. Far be it from me to argue with long standing rules of physics and biology, but when science parts company with God, that's where I get off. After all, there's not a scientist in the world who can make something out of nothing. Yet that's what God did. He made an entire world out of what you see out there. Now, who are you going to believe?''

Tony turned back to his keyboard. ''Sorry for the scare. But, I figured that since we're here, I'd show you the world before God came along. Neat, huh?''

Tie Li thought for a moment. ''I'd rather come from God than science.''

''You did,'' Tony agreed. ''We all did.''

Kim moved to the doorway and stood looking out into the void. He closed his eyes and imagined a world filled with trees and flowers, a land populated with people and animals, all living their lives together in harmony, in love. There were no sounds of battle, of life and death struggles—no screams of victims facing the end. In his mind he saw gentle creatures walking along beside children, lions romping with laughing boys and girls. All was peace. All was life.

"It must have been beautiful," he said, a weariness creeping into his voice. "It must have been so very beautiful."

Tony looked up, a smile creasing his face. Kim now realized something Tony and Tie Li had already learned. The world was not the way it was supposed to be. It was not God's plan for man to live in fear. But there was a plan, a wonderful promise, introduced in Eden. Enmity. That's part of what the Creator had called it. Enmity. When would it come? What would it do? Tony busied himself with the task at hand. They weren't home yet. Time was running out. *Voyager* had to be told what to do.

As Tony worked, Tie Li sat in the doorway of the machine, her feet dangling into the void. Somehow the blackness didn't seem so frightening anymore. After all, this is what God had used to create a world. No, she couldn't understand it. Even Tony's active brain stopped short of comprehending that kind of power. But why should she be afraid of things she didn't understand? God knew what was going on. He would know what to do in any situation. The thought was warm and reassuring. It would make the world with its trees and flowers and people more important to her. It would make God more important to her too.

"Will you look at this!" Tony's voice called out in the stillness. The children glanced over at their brother. Several wires dangled from his outstretched hand. "Here's our problem. Someone pulled these out of their attach points. This is why we had the rebound. Not even SYSCHK caught it. These wires are located in a part of the navigation system that doesn't usually need checking. You see, *Voyager* processes information from this microprocessor on return trips and—" Tony looked over at his companions. "Oh, never mind. I'll just reconnect these and we can get out of here. I'll spare you the explanation."

"Thank you," Kim said with a sigh of relief.

The three prepared to leave the void. Before he closed the door, Kim looked again into the darkness. "I'm not going to miss this place," he said. "I prefer some kind of world, even if it's not perfect, to this kind of nothing."

"Me too," Tie Li agreed. "I will be glad to see my own room again."

Tony smiled as *Voyager* swayed back and forth responding to the commands flowing freely again through the computer systems. They were going home. But a question kept nagging at him from deep inside. Who had pulled the wires? What evil hand had propelled them deep into the void?

The Visit

THE roar of traffic, the clickety-clack of heels on pavement, and the incessant hum of humanity reminded Kim he was nowhere near the peaceful surroundings of Galilee. Even Jerusalem hadn't been this noisy.

Leaning back, the boy gazed up through soaring lines of steel and glass as he stood outside the office building waiting for his appointment with Dr. McFerren. The big clock above the entrance reminded the visitor he was a few minutes early.

The boy sauntered over to a smartly dressed window and studied the colorful displays, each designed to catch the eye of hurried shoppers. Somewhere in the distance a radio blared out a rock tune, adding its rhythmic voice to the tumult.

In the reflection of the window, Kim could see people passing by, heads bent low, hurriedly living their lives amid the chaos of big-city schedules and demands.

The boy sighed. It didn't take him long to start missing the farm. But, Dr. McFerren was a nice man. Kim figured he could endure a visit to the city once a week, at least for a while.

"You like those shoes?" A familiar voice spoke nearby.

"Dr. McFerren," Kim gasped. "What are—oh, am I late?"

The man smiled. "No, you're not late, Kim. I saw you down here from my window and thought I'd join you. This is my favorite shoe store. That's where I got these." Dr. McFerren pointed at his brightly polished loafers. "They gave me a good deal, too. At least they said they did." He laughed out loud. "You never know. I probably could have gotten them $5 cheaper across the street. But, the salesman seemed so sincere. I'm a sucker for sincerity."

Kim admired the doctor's shoes. "They look great and I mean that sincerely."

Dr. McFerren nodded. "Very good, my boy. You're learning."

Kim grinned up at his friend. He liked the doctor's openness, honesty. He knew Dr. McFerren cared about him, about the problems he faced in the world.

"Come Kim, there's someone I want you to meet." The two walked down the street, away from the office building. When the boy questioned as to where they were going, his friend simply teased, "You'll see."

A few blocks later Dr. McFerren turned and ventured into the courtyard of an old brick building. The sign above the gate read "Garden Apartments." Kim didn't see any trace of a garden as he and the doctor moved toward the large doors guarding the entrance to the building.

"What is this place?" Kim asked, searching the dark windows looming above them as they stood waiting for an answer to Dr. McFerren's knock. "It's kinda depressing."

A sullen form appeared at the door. "What do you . . .

oh, Dr. McFerren. It's you. Come on in!" A toothless grin creased the deeply furrowed face of the speaker. "She'll be happy to see you."

The doctor laughed. "I'll bet."

"Oh, don't be that way," the old man at the door said frowning.

"You know she looks forward to your visits."

Dr. McFerren nodded and motioned for Kim to follow. The two made their way along a dark hall and climbed two flights of stairs. "The elevator broke down about eighteen years ago," the doctor said between puffs. "I can't say much for these stairs, either."

Kim noticed a definite sway to the boards underfoot. "About as bad as *Voyager,*" he mumbled.

"Did you say something?" the man asked.

"Oh . . . no . . . I was just thinking out loud."

The doctor smiled. "You'd fit right in here."

A voice called out from a darkened corridor. "Hello Dr. McFerren. Come to see 304 again? Good. Give her my greetings."

"Sure thing Mrs. Jackson. I'll do that."

Another voice filtered through the thin walls. "Thanks for the doughnuts, Dr. McFerren. I liked the lemon ones best."

"To your health, Mr. Bartoski."

"Hey McFerren," yet another voice echoed from behind closed doors. "Thanks for the afghan. My legs are much warmer now." A series of manufactured coughs chased the words down the hall. "I still could use a nice fluffy comforter. You know, like the one across the street in Miller's Dry-Goods Store. I believe it's on sale too!"

"I've got my eye on it, George," Dr. McFerren called back.

"You're a good man," came the reply. "The red one looks the warmest if you ask me."

"My feelings exactly," the doctor replied, winking at Kim.

Other greetings drifted in the stale air. Kim listened as his companion acknowledged each one. It seemed every occupant of the old run-down dwelling had something to say to Dr. McFerren. The man answered each call with encouraging words and a smile. The questioners couldn't see the smile, but they could hear it in the voice coming from the hall.

Finally the man stopped in front of a battered green door. Someone had very carefully painted the numbers "304" in bright gold letters right at eye-level. Dr. McFerren gently knocked.

"Who is it?" came the immediate reply.

"It's me, Willy."

"Willy who?"

"Willy McFerren. You remember me, don't you?" The doctor threw Kim a knowing grin, then continued. "I was here yesterday. We had a nice visit."

The door creaked open an inch or two. Kim could see nothing behind the small crack. "I had no visitors yesterday."

"Sure you did," Dr. McFerren urged. "We had tea. You gave me some oatmeal cookies and we watched your favorite game show. You remember?"

The door opened a little more. "Cookies? Tea? You must have me confused with someone else."

"No, no, no. You just forgot, that's all. May we come in?"

"Who's that?" A crooked finger emerged from the shadows.

170

"This is Kim, my friend. He'd like to visit with you too. If it's not convenient we could come back another time." The man turned as if to leave.

"Nonsense." The door opened wide. "As long as you're here, you may as well come in. And your friend can come in too, I guess."

The room was dark. Shades were pulled tightly, keeping daylight at bay. The doctor walked over to a nearby window and parted the curtains. Sunlight streamed into the small apartment, illuminating the simple chairs and bare wooden floor.

"Aaaahhhh!" Kim jumped as an old wrinkled woman hobbled across the room, her fist shaking in front of her face. "Don't do that!" she shrieked. "What are you trying to do, blind an old woman?"

The doctor ignored the attack. "Sunshine's good for you," he said, throwing back the curtains in the tiny kitchen. "It makes you healthy."

The woman followed, shouting her protest as each darkened window burst with light.

Kim noticed that the tiny apartment was neat and orderly. What furnishings there were showed signs of careful attention as well as wear. Across the couch a colorful bedspread had been tucked in carefully at each corner, the makeshift cover sharing the same design as the neatly folded spread resting at the end of the single metal-frame bed against the far wall of the room.

In the cupboard, flowered teacups grew in orderly rows guarding the plates and saucers stacked behind. Plastic flowers nodded in the breeze flowing through the newly opened windows. Kim figured those were the only kinds of plant life capable of surviving in this sunless world.

"There," Dr. McFerren said, surveying the brightly lit room.

"Isn't that better?"

The old woman sat down in her chair beside the couch, her breath coming in puffs. "First you blind me, then you wear me out. Is that any way for a guest to act?"

"Now, now, don't be angry with me. I'm just trying to look out for you, that's all."

"Well, I've got a husband who does that!" the lady retorted.

"Oh yes, I forgot. How's he doing?"

"Quite well," the woman brightened. "I expect him back any day now. He's on a job down south. He's a hard worker, that man. I don't know what I'd do without him."

Dr. McFerren nodded. "Yes, you've told me. You must be very proud of him."

"Oh I am," the woman sighed. "But, I do miss him when he's gone away so long."

For the next half hour Kim listened as Dr. McFerren talked to the old woman who sat in the chair. She spoke of dreams and plans, of her husband and the house he was going to build for her in the country. Her eyes shone brightly as she hinted of the happy times to come. As words flowed from her lips, the years seemed to fade from her dark, wrinkled skin. There was strength in her dreams. Dr. McFerren understood that.

". . . and I will have a flower garden by the back door. Each day, I'll pick a fresh bouquet for the table. I love flowers. I truly love flowers." The voice grew weak, tired. "Did you know that?"

"Yes," the doctor whispered. "I know. And you love the sound of rain and the smell of baking bread. And you love to hear children singing in church and the chime of your grandmother's clock in the hall. Remember?''

The old woman's head nodded slowly. Her eyes saddened.

"And you love your son. You love him very much. And he loves you very much. Can you remember that, too? Can you?''

The woman's eyes closed, her breathing becoming shallow, slow. Dr. McFerren reached over and gently caressed the old woman's cheek. He hummed softly, a tune he seemed to know well.

"I've got to go now,'' the man said after he finished. He spoke, even though the old woman was asleep. "I'll come again tomorrow. Remember, I love you, Mama.''

Kim looked up in surprise, tears stinging his eyes. The doctor smiled a sad, lonely smile. "She doesn't remember me.'' he said. "The doctors say she may never know who I am. But, I know who I am. I'm her son.''

The man rose and walked around the room quietly closing all the curtains. Darkness captured the tiny dwelling once again. At the door he motioned for Kim to follow. Together they walked along the hallway, down the creaking, swaying stairs, and through the barren courtyard.

At the gate the doctor turned to his companion. "Kim, I won't need to see you anymore. I can tell you've learned the secret of surviving in this world. It's in your eyes when you look at other people, when you look at me. I don't know how you found it, but, it's there.''

"What do you mean Dr. McFerren? What have I found?''

"You've found love, Kim. When someone else's pain can bring tears to your own eyes that means love lives in your heart. I didn't teach you that. Someone else did. My job is to know that it happened.'' The doctor extended his hand. "Have a good life, my friend. I'll send the appropriate papers to your father."

The man turned to leave, but Kim stopped him. "Dr. McFerren. Thank you. Thank you for caring about me."

With a wave the doctor was gone. Kim watched him cross the street and enter Martin's Dry-Goods Store. The boy nodded. Yes, that's exactly what the Nazarene would have done.

With a final glance toward the old apartment building, Kim began walking along the busy sidewalk. The hour was late. He didn't want to keep Mr. Parks waiting.

The Hill

TONY crept through the early-morning calm. The grass felt cold and wet on his bare feet, but he didn't seem to notice. To the east, the first hint of day glowed amber along the horizon.

A cow in the barnyard stirred, watching the silent figure move slowly toward the workshop. The animal voiced its concern with a low "Mooo."

The farm's cocky rooster, used to being the first to rise, was heading for his usual perch on the gatepost to announce the coming day. He jumped sideways in startled surprise when he saw Tony slipping along the fence. Confused, the proud bird spun around and raced back into the chicken house.

Tony stopped and listened. Yes! There it was again! From inside his workshop came a *rat-tat-tat-screech* noise he had heard through his open bedroom window. A sly grin creased Tony's cheeks. The intruder had returned.

High in the big yellow house two sleepy faces appeared at different windows. Tie Li and Kim pressed their noses against the cold glass. They had heard the sounds too and now watched as their brother closed the gap between himself and the workshop door.

Tie Li held her breath, watching Tony's hand slowly reach out and grasp the doorknob. Then with one quick move the boy darted inside.

Nothing happened at first. Then a wild commotion sent them racing down the stairs, bathrobes flying in their wake.

They reached the door to the workshop at the same instant. Breathlessly they gazed into the darkened room. Kim reached up and flipped on the light. Papers, books, electronic equipment, and other items had tumbled from the workbench and lay scattered across the floor.

"Not again!" Tie Li moaned.

"Never again," came the reply from a corner of the room. Tony sat cross-legged on the floor. Beside him a wooden box rested against the wall. From inside the crate came a strange, whirring sound, like an electric blender gone haywire.

Kim eyed the noisy enclosure. "You caught the intruder?" he asked.

"Yup."

"And he fits into an apple box?"

"Yup."

Kim bent down and slowly pulled back one of the boards covering the top of the box. Two flashing eyes surrounded by a dark mask stared back at him.

"It's an animal!" Kim gasped. "And a strange-looking one at that."

Tie Li joined her brother. "It look like a furry burglar."

"That's exactly what it is," Tony agreed, painfully rising to his feet. "I can't think of a better way to describe a raccoon."

"He *cute!*" Tie Li squealed.

"That 'cute' thing sent us all into the void. Those little furry fingers were the ones that pulled the wires in *Voyager*. And that sweet little bundle of energy trashed my workshop"—the boy looked around the room—"twice!"

The raccoon trilled angrily.

"You think that's hilarious, don't you?" Tony snapped, addressing the animal. "Well, I've got a news flash for you, you crazy wrecking machine. Let's see how funny you think it is when I let you loose 20 miles from here, out in the middle of nowhere."

Kim snickered. "He'll love it."

"I know," Tony blushed. "I'm a real meanie, aren't I?"

Tie Li giggled. "He probably take the bus back."

"I wouldn't doubt it," Tony said, passing a strong rope around the box. "Let's get Dad. He'll drive us over to Bartin County. Lots of raccoon country out there. Maybe this crazy furball will fall in love with some other masked burglar and stay away forever. We can only hope."

After lifting the raccoon-filled apple box onto the back of the farm pickup truck, the children headed for the big yellow house. The mystery had been solved. Now *Voyager* could make future journeys without the reprogramming offered by this furry forest friend.

* * *

Grandmother looked up in surprise. "A raccoon did all that?"

Tie Li nodded. "It was big mess."

Tony walked from the kitchen, a glass of milk in one hand and a plate of warm peanut butter cookies in the other. "He was probably looking for food or something," he said, seating himself by the fireplace. "Oh, well, he's history. I wouldn't be surprised if he's raiding some unsuspecting cabin in Bartin County at this very moment.''

Grandmother smiled. ''I wish I could have seen him.''

''We can go bring him back,'' Kim offered. ''I'm sure he loves cookies too.''

''Never mind,'' Grandmother laughed. ''We'll let him bother someone else for a while. We mustn't be selfish.''

The children sat in silence for a few moments enjoying the sweet, tasty treat Grandmother had baked. Their ''mmm's'' and ''ahhh's'' were the old woman's reward for her thoughtfulness.

''So,'' she said after the last crumb had disappeared, ''what's happening with your machine, Tony? Where are you off to next?''

The boy became serious. ''To Jerusalem,'' he said. ''It's time for the Passover.''

Grandmother glanced at her grandson, then at the others. ''Oh. I see,'' she said quietly.

''I can't believe what the Book says happened,'' Tony continued. ''It doesn't make sense. Why would they do that?''

Tie Li looked up at her brother. ''Do what, Tony? What happened in Jerusalem?''

Kim studied Tony's face. ''Whatever it is, it's not pleasant, is it?''

''No,'' Tony admitted, ''it's not pleasant at all.''

''Do we have to see it?'' Kim asked. ''Can't we just go someplace else?'' Grandmother placed her hand on Kim's shoulder and addressed the children. ''Come back here on your return. We'll talk about it, OK?''

The three nodded. Quietly they made their way out of the cabin and followed the path leading to the farm. Tony looked up at the sunlight streaming through the trees. How could he explain it to his brother and sister? He felt a growing fear deep in his chest.

* * *

Jerusalem swarmed with activity. In every corner of the city, travelers moved along the crowded streets, searching for places to stay and food to eat. In the distance the white-gold gleam of the Temple dominated the scene—and the thoughts of each visitor. Passover was a time of remembrance, a time to reflect on God's deliverance, a time to be thankful.

The children made their way through the city, Tony in the lead. He said nothing. Kim and Tie Li wondered what could make their brother so sad with all the joyous celebration going on around them.

Their journey led them through tall, stately gates and along a busy thoroughfare outside the city walls. Here the crowds thinned a little. But something else was changing too. Instead of shouts of greeting and happy conversations, the children heard voices raised in anger and someone barking orders. Through it all a steady *thud, thud, thud* reverberated in the warm air.

The road wound up a steep hill. At the summit, the children saw tall Roman soldiers standing in a circle, motioning toward something on the ground. A crowd had gathered nearby, shouting encouragement to the soldiers. One of the helmeted men was on his knees, pounding a large spike. A long piece of wood jutted from between the feet of another soldier.

"They build something?" Tie Li asked, straining to see. "Tony? They build a house here?"

The boy didn't answer. Tie Li noticed that her brother was searching the faces of the crowd standing on the other side of the soldiers. His eyes focused on a small group huddled together at the front of the gathering. "Oh, no," he whispered. "She *is* here."

Tie Li and Kim followed his gaze to a woman whose face was buried in the chest of a big, bearded man. "There Peter," the little girl said, pointing. The woman in the big man's arms looked toward the soldiers, her face twisted in agony.

"Isn't that Mary, the Nazarene's mother?" Kim asked. "I remember her from before."

"Yes," Tony answered. "And those are the disciples."

"Tony, what's going on here? Why is Mary crying?" Kim looked at his brother. "Where's Jesus? Where's the Nazarene?" He was beginning to sense something was terribly wrong.

The soldiers bent down and started to lift something heavy from the ground. It was the long plank of wood. As the burden cleared the circle of men, the children saw another plank crossing the first near the top. But wait! There was something on the wood. It was a man! There was a man on the wood! Tony, Tie Li, and Kim stepped back in horror. The man's hands and feet had long metal spikes driven through them. Higher and higher the structure was lifted. The soldiers strained, one holding the end of the plank on the ground. A deep hole had been dug at his feet. He was going to slide the plank into that hole.

Tie Li gasped as the full realization of what she was witnessing washed over her. The face of the man nailed to the wood was grotesquely deformed with pain. Higher, higher he went. Blood ran down his sides and legs.

The plank teetered at the top of its climb as the soldier at its base wrestled it toward the hole in the ground. Then, with a wrenching thud, it dropped into position. Flesh tore along the hanging man's hands and feet as his full weight tugged at the spikes. His body swung out away from the planks, then suddenly slammed back against them as the structure settled into its foundation.

A cheer rose from the crowd. Fists waved in the air. Voices shouted, "We have no king but Caesar! We have no king but Caesar!"

Tie Li cried out, her body shaking, "Tony, Kim, that Jesus! That man up there is Jesus!"

A long branch bristling with sharp thorns formed a twisted crown around the Nazarene's head. Puncture wounds dotted his face as the makeshift crown scraped against the wood behind him.

Kim felt sick, dizzy. He looked toward the disciples. Mary stood gazing up at her bleeding, dying son. Her lips moved. Kim recognized the unspoken words. "Jeshua, Jeshua." Then she collapsed in Peter's arms.

Tie Li fell to her knees, tears streaming down her thin face. "Why?" she screamed. "Why they do this? He not hurt anyone. He not bad person. Why they do this to him?"

Tony walked toward the cross, his eyes on the man hanging high above. He heard the soldiers laughing and joking with one another. He noticed two other men were being dragged up the hill. Two other crosses waited on the ground.

Tony glanced up at the outstretched hands, now swollen and turning blue as the lifeblood flowed from them. An image of a little boy holding his palm up to his father flashed through his mind. "It hurt, Daddy, it hurt." The tiny voice echoed in his memory. Where was the father now? Would there be no one to comfort the man on the cross?

Tony glanced at the crowd. How could these people do

this to the Son of God? Didn't they know? Didn't they want to know?

"Father." A strained, gurgling voice called softly above the boy. Tony looked up to see the man trying to lift his head. "Father," the Nazarene repeated, the effort racking his body with convulsions, "why . . . have You . . . forsaken me?"

Tony turned toward his companions. They stood holding each other, sobbing, their faces ashen. "Come on," he said quickly. "Let's get out of here."

The three made their way down the hill to where *Voyager* waited. Before entering the machine, they turned and gazed toward the distant hill. Now three crosses stood against the sky. Behind them storm clouds were building, shutting out the sun. Tony shook his head in disbelief. Even heaven was drawing a curtain across the awful scene.

Why? Why was the Saviour of mankind, the Creator of the earth, the only power willing to take on Satan, hanging up there on the hill? Had the serpent won? Was there no hope after all?

The door to *Voyager* closed. Burning questions hung in the minds of the travelers as the machine disappeared from view.

Master Plan

THE children ate very little that evening. The memory was still too fresh, too painful in their minds.

After the supper dishes had been washed and the chores completed, Tony, Tie Li, and Kim walked through the gathering twilight along the path leading to the little cabin in the clearing. Grandmother would be waiting. Maybe she'd know the reasons for the terrible scene they had witnessed. So many questions crowded their thoughts. Why would an innocent, kind, loving God allow the very people He created to kill Him? The whole idea seemed senseless, totally beyond reason.

Grandmother was waiting at the front door. She smiled and hugged each child warmly. "Thank you for coming back," she said. "I think we need to talk about this."

Tony flopped down on the large beanbag by the fireplace. "It was even worse than I imagined. His mother was there. The disciples too. They all just stood and watched. There wasn't anything they could do."

Kim nodded. "The crowd had hate in their eyes. I've seen that look before. Why did they hate Him so? He was only trying to help everybody.''

A sob came from the end of the couch where Tie Li sat. ''Nobody help Him. Nobody.''

Grandmother listened as the children recounted what they had seen. She sat in silence, letting the awful story fill the room like a choking smoke.

When they had finished, the old woman hesitated for a long moment, clarifying in her own mind how she would address the terrible event the children had witnessed. When she finally spoke, her words were carefully chosen.

''Many, many thousands of years ago, before this earth was created, Satan made a very serious accusation. It was a lie, really. But one third, *one third,* of all the angels in heaven believed him. Satan said it was impossible for any man or any woman to live a life according to God's plan. He also accused God of being a tyrant, a dictator, and said that created beings served Him out of fear, not love.

''So when Jesus formed this world, Satan was right there pointing his finger at Him saying, 'Let's see who's right, shall we? Let me tempt these beings, and I'll prove that my statements are true.'

''God knew how powerful evil could be. So eons before Creation He and His Son designed a plan—a master plan that would prove Satan wrong. That plan . . . would assure that evil's hold on this earth would one day be forever broken. That plan . . . was Jesus.''

Kim sat forward in his chair. ''I get it. He came to earth to show us that God was really our friend, that we could trust Him after all.''

''That's right,'' Grandmother encouraged, ''But there is more.'' Turning to Tony and Tie Li, she added, ''Do you remember what He said to the serpent in Eden after Adam and Eve had eaten the fruit?''

"Enmity!" Tony shouted. "He said there would be something that would finally destroy Satan."

"Exactly," Grandmother said enthusiastically. "That something is God's incredible love for you. That's why He took our punishment and died for us. He couldn't bear the thought of heaven without us.

"When Jesus showed the people of His time how to live a life free from sin, they didn't like it—they felt guilty every time they heard Him speak. So they looked for ways to get rid of Him. Not everyone was like that, you understand, but enough were. Eventually, as you saw, they had Him killed.

"And one more thing. Only a God who has conquered sin can forgive sin."

"But," Tie Li said with a sigh, "Jesus is dead. Sin did win after all."

"Yeah," Kim nodded. "What good is a forgiving God if He's dead?"

Grandmother turned to Tony. "Haven't you told them?"

"Told them what?"

The old woman's eyes opened wide. "The rest of the story . . . what happened next. Didn't you read it?"

"I stopped reading the Book when Jesus was killed. I didn't want to find out any more. I was too sad."

"Tony, Tie Li, Kim! You don't know what happened two days later?" Grandmother looked astounded.

The children shook their heads.

Grandmother Parks fairly flew across the room. Grabbing the Book off the shelf, she hurried over to Tony. "Here," she said excitedly thumbing through the pages, "read . . . this. Just read it!"

Tony took the Book and scanned the words. His eyes grew wide in amazement, and his mouth dropped open.

"Grandmother," he gasped, "I didn't know. I didn't know!"

"Didn't know what?" Kim and Tie Li chorused.

"Come on!" Tony jumped up and raced out of the cabin. The other children ran behind, stumbling through the dark. Grandmother shouted after them, her voice echoing through the forest. "It's the best part, *the best part of all!*"

The door to the workshop flew open as Tony burst into the room. Heading straight to his computer, he began typing furiously.

Kim and Tie Li arrived just as their brother jumped into his machine. "Come on, you guys. Hurry! You're not going to believe it. Come on!"

In moments, *Voyager* flashed white and disappeared. On the computer screen resting above the workbench a group of words glowed in the darkness.

DESTINATION CODE: TOMB (JOSEPH OF ARI-MATHEA)

TIME: SUNDAY (DAWN)

COORDINATES: 24U2/3OII9-JERUSALEM

VOYAGER: UNDERWAY—CONDITION (NOR-MAL)

The early-morning sun was just peeking over the horizon as *Voyager* settled gently on the grassy slope of a garden nestled on the outskirts of Jerusalem. As the light radiating from the machine faded, its door swung open, spilling three children onto the ground.

Tony looked around, his gaze falling on an opening in the face of a stone wall about 20 feet away. "Over there," he called to his companions. "That must be it."

"What is *it?*" Kim asked, following behind his brother. "What are we looking for?"

"The tomb. The place where they buried Jesus."

"Hey!" Tie Li stopped in her tracks. "I don't want to see tomb."

"Yes, you do," Tony urged. "Believe me, you do!"

When the three reached the opening, Tony bent low and crept inside. Kim and Tie Li stayed behind, resting on a large, round stone lying on the ground.

In a few seconds Tony returned, a look of wonder and joy spreading across his face.

"What is it?" Kim asked, afraid of what the answer might be. "What's in there?"

"See for yourself," the younger boy encouraged.

Tie Li took hold of Kim's arm as they entered the tomb.

The two returned, puzzled. "So," Kim mumbled, "there's nothing in there. What's so great about that?"

Tony closed his eyes, savoring each word as he spoke. "This is the tomb where they buried Jesus."

"Well, where's the body? There's nothing in there."

A thought began to surface in Tie Li's mind. She remembered the story of the widow's son, the one Tony had told her. The prophet Elijah had raised the young boy from the . . . the . . .

"Tony," the girl cried, "is He, is He . . .?" She dared not say it for fear she was wrong.

"Yes! He has risen. *He's alive!*" Tony jumped up and down. "The Book said He rose early this morning. Kim, Tie Li, the Nazarene is alive again! He did it. *He did it!* He beat death. Satan is *not* stronger after all. Now He can forgive. Now He can help us all. Do you know what that means?"

Kim nodded. "That means we don't have to be afraid of Satan or death or anything."

Tony turned and ran toward *Voyager*. "We've got to tell

people what happened. They'll want to know what we've seen."

"No, wait," Kim called. "They won't believe us. Besides, this all happened a couple thousand years ago. They'll just say we're kids with wild imaginations. Hey, Jesus Himself couldn't get more than a handful of people to listen to Him when He was here in person."

"Maybe so," Tony countered. "But the Book, it has a lot more pages in it. I haven't read them all, but I've heard stories. Grandmother used to tell me about a man named Paul who traveled all around on boats and stuff. He had exciting adventures telling people about Jesus. Peter the fisherman and some of the other disciples wrote about what they did too. Now I understand why. Everybody needs forgiveness. Because the Nazarene isn't in that tomb, He can do what He said He'd do. He can give people hope again."

Tony waved toward the city. "So what if not everybody in our time believes. If just a few listen, that'll be all right with me. We can do like the Nazarene did. We can *live* with love in our hearts. We can be kind to other people, help them. Then they'll listen. I'm sure they will."

Kim nodded. "It's worth a try."

The children hurried toward *Voyager*. "By the way," Kim asked, "if Jesus isn't in the tomb, where is He? I mean, where is He in our time?"

Tony entered the machine and began flipping switches. "I don't know. But I'll find out. He can't be very far away. He always seems to show up at the right time."

Tie Li looked up at her brother, a satisfied smile on her face. "Tony," she said, "we see Him again someday."

Tony glanced down at the girl in surprise. "Why do you say that, little sister?"

"I don't know. Just a feeling."

The younger boy reached up to pull the door closed. His eye caught the first ray of morning as it flooded the opening of the tomb with a golden light. "You're probably right," he said. "And when it happens, it'll be something to see."

Voyager faded from view, leaving the garden as empty as the tomb. Beyond the trees, Jerusalem stirred. A new day was dawning.